Candle Dark

Book One - Ironbridge Gorge Series

For Elizabeth

Carole Anne Carr

i

Cover illustration by the artist Sophie Bignall
sophiebignall@hotmail.com

Cover Design by James Brinkler
info@jamesbrinkler.co.uk

Published by Carole Anne Carr

Inside illustrations by the Author

Website: http://caroleannecarr.co.uk
Email: carole@caroleannecarr.com

ISBN: 978-0-9559818-1-4

Carole Anne Carr
Shropshire
Children's Author

Member of the Society of Authors

National Association of Writers in Education

B.Ed.Hons. (PrimaryEd)
Dip.Ed. (Medieval History)
HDTheology (Worc.)
HD Child.Lit. (Open)

First Wolf
Book One - Wolf Series

It was Toland's twelfth year of life when his father hurled the wolf's head at the mighty Eorl Uhtred, bringing his childhood to a violent end.

These were dangerous times, with people driven from their settlements, tribal wars, and bands of robbers on the roads, but Toland must keep his solemn promise to save the Lindisfarne Gospels from the Vikings, protect his family, and find his father.

With his faithful hound Bodo, he sets off on his quest through Anglo-Saxon Northumbria. Surviving the first Viking attack of Lindisfarne, his many adventures lead him to the mysterious hermit on Inner Farne, Bamburgh fortress, the slave girl Kendra, the mystery of the stolen jewels, a blood debt, and a terrible discovery at the White Church.....

Synopsis

Joshua was nearly eleven and he'd worked down the Blists Hill coal pit since he was seven and a bit. He hated it down there. He hated working in the dark, he hated the rats and the stink of the tunnels, and he especially hated it when the mine flooded and his wet boots rubbed his feet raw.

Then on the day that Bradley the horsekeeper gave him another beating so bad he ached all over, he made up his mind to run away and find work on the Severn trows. But what would happen to poor Drummer, left behind in the dark? What would happen to his mum and sisters if he left them to the mercy of the evil Isaac Whitlock? And how could he sail to Bristol, when his dad had been set to work in the most dangerous part of the mine?

Afraid of the river gangs and worrying about his dad, Joshua must decide whether to run for his life, or to stay in Coalport and try to protect his family.

This book is written for the children who accompanied me to the Blists Hill Victorian Village on many environmental study trips - often having to remove snow from their clipboards and huddle in the Toll House for warmth. They remained cheerful, despite the difficult conditions, and the work they produced was a delight.

Historical Note

Candle Dark describes the lives of children who worked in coalmines in England in the late 18th century, and the story is set in and around the Ironbridge Gorge, Shropshire. At that time, Blists Hill was a remote mining community and the nearby village of Coalport was gradually acquiring commercial importance after the building of the Preens Eddy Bridge.

Although the characters and events are imaginary, I have tried to reflect the working conditions, and the life of a family, living in the Gorge at this time of rapid industrial growth - a period in history that was later to be known as the Industrial Revolution.

Contents

One – The Worst Day of My Life

Two – Falling into the Dark

Three – Creaking and Groaning

Four – A Stone by the Door

Five – A Terrible Sight!

Six – A Day of the Fair that Wasn't

Seven – The Time for Running Away

Eight – Sam

Nine – Sam has an Idea

Ten — No Way Out!

Eleven – Wild with Anger

Twelve — Blood, Birds, and Butterflies

Thirteen – Betrayal

Fourteen – Thunder

Fifteen – Dangerous Heights

Sixteen – A Ghost in the Warehouse

Seventeen – A Promise Made

x

1

The Worst Day of My Life

 'Is it a rat?' Sara cried, 'tell it to go away, Josh!'

I woke with a start from my nightmare about falling down a mineshaft, and in the dull red glow coming through our bedroom window, I saw my four-year-old sister. She'd tangled herself up in an old petticoat Mum puts on her at bedtime. We sleep on the floor and our beds are potato sacks stuffed with hay. Sara shares hers with my big sister Maria, on the other side of the room from me.

'Go to sleep, Sara,' I muttered crossly. 'There isn't any rat.'

'It's going to eat me,' she wailed. She was sitting up, clutching her peg doll. Tears were dripping off her chin.

I sighed. I could hear what sounded like an animal pressing its nose into its fur and snuffling, searching for fleas. I felt for my boot, flung it, and the snuffling stopped.

'There, it's gone. No more crying – let me sleep.' I punched the hay in my sack, trying to make the lumpy bits comfortable, but it was no good, I was wide-awake.

Oh, I'm Joshua Hale, but everyone calls me Josh, and the terrible thing I'm going to tell you about happened when I was nearly eleven. I'd worked down the Blists Hill coal pit since I was seven and I hated it down there. I hated working in the dark. I hated the rats, the stink of the tunnels, and I hated it when the mine flooded and my wet boots rubbed my feet raw.

I was scared in the pit most days, but Dad said we all had to work to pay rent for our cottage, find money to give to the tommy shop for his new pick, and to buy food. Mum said if we didn't have enough money for rent, the mine manager would turn us out in the road. Then we'd end up in the workhouse.

But yesterday, when Bradley the horsekeeper gave me another beating so bad I ached all over, I decided I'd had enough. I would run away, find work on the river, and earn lots of money. Then Mum needn't take things that Isaac Whitlock gave her when he came knocking at our door. Thinking of Isaac made me shudder, and I was wondering about the best time to run away when Sara started her mithering again.

'Maria won't play with me,' she whined.

Maria had her face to the wall. She'd pulled the old blanket tight over her head. Sara was dancing her peg doll along her sister's arm and poking the peg through the holes in the cover.

'Maria's tired,' I warned Sara. 'Let her sleep or she'll thump you.'

'The rat's going to bite me.'

'There's nothing to be feared of, it won't get you. I'm here. I won't let it.' That seemed to content her. I saw her rub her eyes with her small fists and curl up on the outside of the blanket, her thumb stuck in her mouth.

At night, the fiery glow from the furnaces and burning coal heaps around the Dale filled our small bedroom, but now the grey light of dawn was growing stronger. I could hear the goodly noise of birds chirping in the woods on our side of the valley, but coming closer was another sound I *didn't* like.

It was the knocker-up man, his boots crunching on the road as he tapped his long pole on the bedroom windows of the cottages. Every day except Sundays, he shouted at the workers to get out of bed and I groaned because it must be turned four already. There'd be no more sleep for me now.

Grumbling to myself, I picked up my clothes from the floor and they twitched, making me drop them in a hurry. A long sleek furry animal wriggled from under my shirt and bounced away.

Flattening its body, it squeezed through the gap under our bedroom door and pattered softly downstairs. Sara had been going on about a rat, but it was just Dad's ferret escaped from its cage in the yard. I wondered how it had lifted the catch and got out.

Muttering angrily to myself, for Sara had woken me for nothing, I struggled to push my legs into my trousers. They were a pair of Dad's old ones, cut down to fit me, stiff with coal dust. They felt horribly damp, but my shirt was warm where the ferret had slept in it. Forcing my bare feet into my boots was like standing in icy water. I was glad I had Dad's old jacket, it would be cold out there in the early mist before the sun was fully up.

Clumping across the floor, I bent down, shaking Maria by the shoulder. She cussed me, pulling the blanket tighter over her head. I wasn't too bothered if I woke Sara. She wasn't bothered about waking me. There'd be another four hours before *she'd* have to be up. She wouldn't be set to work when she was seven, as I was. Mum would try to keep her home a bit longer. Sara was Mum's favourite.

When I went into the kitchen, Mum was putting bowls on the scrubbed wooden table. Our porridge was bubbling in the iron pot over the cooking range fire. Mum had lit the smoky oil lamp on the dresser. It was still dark in there with only one small

4

window.

Dad was sitting on the bench with his elbows on the table. Mum said I looked a lot like him. We had the same straw-coloured hair. I was skinny like Dad, but he walked with a stoop.

 He said it was from all those years working in the mine.

'Morning,' I said, sliding along the bench beside him.

I watched Mum lift the big pan from the kitchen range and ladle the thick porridge into bowls. I always hoped I'd get a lot. I loved the warm kitchen, the feeling of hot porridge going down inside me, and seeing Mum busy and wearing the apron she'd made from her old dress with the yellow flowers on it.

This was the best time of all when I listened to the coals falling in the grate, feeling comfortable and safe. It was awful when breakfast was over and I had to go to work.

'I need you to fetch water after work, Josh,' Mum said, pushing my bowl towards me. 'The buckets are nearly empty.'

'Can't Maria do it? It's not fair, it's *her* turn,' I said. I grabbed my spoon, digging it into the steaming porridge.

'Maria's got to help *me*. Do as you're told for once, Josh, will

5

you,' Mum sighed.

I grumbled under my breath, but I knew by the way Mum pressed her lips together she wouldn't change her mind. I didn't want a clip round the ear. I always had to do the heavy work, like carrying water from the pump. There'd be the privy bucket to empty too, after I'd fetched coal from the shed.

'I told you about that muttering,' Mum said. 'Where's Maria? Did you wake her? You'd best be quick go see, or she'll be late for work.'

I didn't need to, for I heard her boots thumping on the stairs, and when she came in the kitchen, you couldn't tell if Maria was a lad or a girl with her work clothes on. She'd pushed her long hair under her hat, her face almost hidden by the torn brim. She wore a pair of Dad's old trousers, one of his shirts, and a jacket the vicar's wife had given to Mum, now black with coal dust.

'Morning,' I said, but she ignored me.

Marching across the brick floor in boots that were too big for her, she slid along the bench, pulling her porridge bowl towards her. She hated work as much as I did, so most times she was angry. She was fifteen. She'd been shovelling coal into the sieve, sorting the big lumps from the rubbish that wouldn't burn, for nearly eight years. She was stronger than I was, but I was fast catching up.

6

She worked on the bank because they don't let girls down the Blists Hill coal pit, as I've heard they do at other mines. I was jealous of her because she was outside all day, not shut underground in the dark like Dad and me. But I couldn't feel bad about Maria for long. When I was little, she used to stick up for me, thumping the bigger lads when they bullied me.

I watched Mum spooning just the right amount of tea leaves into the jug. Our family never said much in the mornings. I didn't mention the ferret because I was worried Dad would think I'd let it out. There was another thing keeping me quiet. By the look on Dad's face, something was bothering him a lot. He was pushing his spoon about in his porridge, not gobbling it down as usual and it didn't seem right.

'They're opening the old mine workings today,' he said suddenly, putting down his spoon and looking hard at Mum. 'I'm one of those as has to work there.'

Mum made a startled clucking noise with her tongue. 'It isn't safe,' she said. She banged the kettle on the hob. Spots of hot water sizzled and splashed, making us jump back a bit on our bench. 'Those workings have been shut up too long – it's ten years or more since the men died down there – it isn't decent. They should have left it closed. There'll be lots of bad air in the tunnels after all this long time.'

7

'It's all right, Hannah, it is safe enough,' Dad said. 'There's no gas they tell us, and they've pumped out the water. Things will be better when they drive a tunnel into the side of the gorge at Coalport. They're going to build a canal to bring the coal out by tub boat, straight from the coalface to the river.'

'It might take years to build such a thing,' Mum said sharply, brushing back hair from her face with a quick movement of her hand. She attacked the loaf with the bread knife. 'Anyway, what has that to do with *you* working with a candle? There's going to be another explosion before long. There's sure to be lots of fire damp–'

'Don't take on so, they say it's safe as houses.'

'If it's as safe as *this* house, then you're in trouble, George Hale. What with the broken window, the roof needing mending, and the mine manager doing nothing.'

'If they use tub boats to bring out the coal, what will happen to Drummer?' I asked. I was worried, but Mum glared at me so I kept quiet.

Mum was still angry when she gave us our food with our tin cannikins. I put my cloth full of bread and cheese in one pocket and picked up my cannikin of tea. I was hoping Mum had put in a carrot with my bread and cheese. I didn't dare ask, she was in such a bad mood, but when we left the kitchen, she gave Dad an

8

extra kiss on the cheek. Then she gave me a very hard hug. Maria had one too, so I knew Mum wasn't angry with us, just worrying about explosions in the old workings.

Dad led the way through the front room and opened the door. Maria and me followed him onto the pit road. I was anxious not to be late. I didn't want a beating from Bradley. Then I remembered I was going to run away. There wouldn't be many more days to be fearful of Bradley's fists.

2

Falling into the Dark

I closed the front door behind us. Dad carried his pick. I held Maria's cannikin, sieve, and shovel while she wrapped a bit of sacking round her belly for an apron. Then glaring at me from under her hat, she snatched her things and strode off to join her

friends, leaving me to walk with Dad.

Our hamlet was half way up the side of the gorge, close to the Coalport Road, and surrounded by trees. Our home was the middle one in a long row of red brick cottages that all looked the same. Every morning, except for Sundays, we joined the other men, women, and children on their way through the woods to the pit bank. We didn't say much to each other. We were all too tired from the long hours working in the mine, but you could hear the crunching of our boots as we tramped up the stony track.

Last winter's gales had felled many of the oak trees, so it was easy for me to look down the hill to see Coalport village and the river running through the valley. A pale sunlight was breaking through the mist, making the slate roofs of the riverside cottages shine. I was glad the wind had changed direction. It had blown away the smoke, fumes, and muck from the blast furnaces. For once, it was easier to breathe.

That morning the Severn brimmed with floodwater, carrying mud, small bushes, and a dead sheep along with it. Dad was hurrying up the path beside the old plateway, but I stopped to watch the sheep. It was spinning round in a whirlpool and I wanted to see what would happen to it.

I'd been down to Coalport village in the gorge a few times, but we didn't mix with the people there. They didn't like us pit bank folk, they called us bad names. Dad said the Coalport people were stuck up, thinking themselves better than they were, especially those who worked in the new pottery.

I could see the big warehouse at the end of the quay with its doors wide open to the slipway, ready for business. I always felt excited when I looked down at the barges and the larger square-rigged trows along the quay. Some trows had covers on their sails, sitting high in the water, waiting for loading. Wisps of smoke rose from the small chimneystacks pushing through the decking on one or two barges. I wondered if the men were cooking breakfast and if they were having porridge same as me.

It was good to think I'd soon be sailing down to Bristol. I was wondering what life would really be like on a trow when I heard the faint chugging of a steam engine starting up. It was coming from the direction of the canal behind the pit bank sheds, and scared I'd be late for work, I scrambled up the hill after Dad.

'Tub boats must be on their way to the Severn already,' Dad said with a heavy sigh, when I caught up with him. 'They're making an early start, mine manager must be about.'

I nodded, though I wasn't really listening. I was looking back down the hill, trying to see what would happen to the sheep, when I noticed one of the larger trows on her way downstream. She was through the new Wood Bridge, the crew working hard to winch up her mast, the wind tugging at her clay-coated sails.

'Look, Dad,' I cried, shaking his jacket sleeve. 'Isn't that the *Emily Grey*? The trow you were first mate on?'

Dad shaded his eyes. 'No, that isn't the *Emily*, she's not big enough. She might be the *Adventurer*, but my eyesight's not as good as it used to be. I can't be sure from here.'

'What's she carrying?' I asked.

'Don't know, probably taking pig iron from the furnace at

Bedlam to Worcester. The Severn's tidal further downstream. That trow's too small to navigate the rougher waters. She won't sail beyond Worcester. With her pig iron unloaded, they'll turn her round. Then she'll come back up river with goods that the bigger ketch-rigged trows have carried from Bristol. She'll be loaded with chests full of tea, coffee, bales of beautiful cloth – barrels of wine and brandy. Not for the likes of us, just for the rich folk in these parts.'

He'd told me that many times. About sailing ships that crossed the seas, bigger than the biggest trows, and about barges carrying groceries and barrels of fish to the riverside villages. I was proud of my dad. He'd been a waterman when he was young, sailing down to the big port of Bristol. Sometimes he told me stories about his life on the river. How he'd hoped to buy a small barge and be an owner, carrying coal and pig iron up as far as Welshpool, but it had never happened.

'Why did you stop working on the trows?' I asked him. I knew the answer by heart, but I always liked to hear him say how he gave up working as a waterman for us. He never seemed tired of the telling.

'When I was a lad, a bit older than you are now, I met your mum. She lived in Coalbrookdale. She was from a family that had a bit of money. Her lot didn't think me fit for their daughter, me being a waterman and her working at the big house, but she married me despite that. Then your sister Maria came along. After that, we had you and Sara. It was long days on the river and I didn't like leaving your mum to manage on her own. Besides, we had nowhere to live. We were all cramped up, sharing with your mum's parents.'

He sighed. He always sighed when he got to that bit and looked miserable. 'So I took work in the mine because the owner was building cottages. We would have a place of our own to live.'

I thought about this and how much I loved Dad because he'd given up sailing on the river to work down the mine in the dark, just for us. Then I shuddered. I'd suddenly remembered Dad was going to the old workings. I lifted my head to the thin sunlight to let it warm my face, wishing we'd never get to the pit bank.

It would be a nicely fresh day. I felt worse on those sorts of days. There'd be little sun left when work was over and the birds were chirruping their evening song. Then remembering that tomorrow was Sunday, the day Mum made a big dinner, I felt cheered. There'd be time to play marbles and swim in the old clay pit when I'd done helping with the household chores. I was planning to hide in the woods and miss going to Sunday school.

We were close to the pit bank now so I gave one last look at the *Adventurer* as the strong river current carried her towards the bend in the river at Sutton Wharf. One of my favourite daydreams was to imagine I was aboard the *Emily Grey*. But this time I pretended I was on the *Adventurer,* shouting orders to my crew as I steered her skilfully downstream.

Placing my hand on the smooth wood of her tiller, I watched the wind filling her sails and guided her carefully out into the deepest part of the river. Avoiding the clumsy barges, dipping and swaying at their moorings, I saw another bridge ahead. I was warning the crew to be ready with the lines, when I heard someone shouting my name. Startled, and brought hurriedly out of my daydream, I realised it was Dad telling me to hurry up.

I trudged miserably after him, my boots sinking in the thick

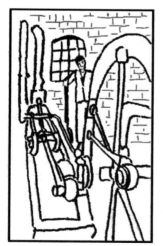

layers of coal dust. Grey smoke billowed from the boiler-shed chimney, the choking bitter fumes making me cough. Next to the shed, the engine house had its door slightly open. I could hear blasts of scalding, hissing steam from the winding engine, and it always excited and frightened me.

Seeing Dad talking to another man, I quickly climbed up the heaps of waste coal to the top of the pit bank and peered in through the gap in the shed door. Sniffing the strong smell of hot oil, I watched the man in charge of the winding engine wiping his hands on a rag. Then turning a wheel on the big pipe, coming through the wall from the boiler in the shed next door, he released the scalding steam into the engine.

I backed away from the whooshing noise, but although I was fearful, I loved the power of the thing. Putting my face close to the door again, I watched nervously as the steam sent the shiny piston slamming backwards and forwards. The heavy flywheel thundered round so fast I could hardly see the spokes. The ground started to shake under me, the iron chain wound round the drum at a terrible speed, and the deep rumbling sound went

right through me.

Looking up, I saw the chain from the drum snaking fast from the hole in the engine house wall, high above my head. It was travelling to the bottom of the pit bank, sliding over the small wheel on top of the wooden pithead gear, and rapidly bringing up one of the first wagons of the day. Then I heard the brake go on in the engine house and I saw an empty coal wagon rise slowly out of the deep hole in the ground.

16

It stopped level with the top of the pit shaft, swinging gently over the gaping hole. The thought of having to climb into it, and hurtle down in the dark, always made me sick in my belly. Worst of all, I knew Bradley the horsekeeper would be waiting for me. But it was time to work, and I was reluctantly sliding down the heaps of coal when I heard Dad shout, 'Quick, Josh, it's the *Emily,* it's the *Emily Grey.*'

My heart beat so fast at the sight of the enormous trow that for a moment I forget my fear of the mine. Through a gap in the trees, I could see the craft's mainsail and mizzen, furled and held securely along the spars. Her prow was cutting through the strong current, causing a steady wash along her beautifully varnished elm planking.

On the riverbank, a team of grunting, sweating men, wearing harnesses like oxen at the plough, were dragging the heavy craft upriver towards Coalport. They were stretching their bodies forward with their hands almost touching the ground. Straining chests, shoulders, bellies they fought the huge weight of her, their violent curses carrying horribly through the gorge.

'Those men are a drunken, thieving lot. They prefer stealing from trows instead of finding honest employment. You'd best keep clear of them, lad,' Dad said with a disgusted grunt. 'Most boat owners will be using horses, once the towpath is finished.

17

But those men will hang about the gorge, seeing what they can steal when their use is long gone. Speaking of thieving, you keep clear of Isaac Whitlock – I've heard he's planning something bad. I know he carries a knife. Men say he killed a lad who was going to tell on him, buried him in the mine!'

Hearing him talk about Isaac, I thought I'd risk asking Dad about something that had been bothering me a lot. I'd heard him having angry words with Mum about Isaac many times when they thought me asleep. I was desperate to find out why.

'Why does Mum say Isaac is a good man?' I said, puzzled.

'Mum would say that. Isaac brings her twists of tea, sugar, bits of nice smelling soap. Not like the ash and pig fat she has to boil up to make soap for us. Don't you go believing the man when he says he's a distant cousin, with no family of his own to give to. It's a pack of lies!'

Dad's tired face had a hard, angry look, so I thought it best not to ask more. When I was the master of my own trow, Mum would have no need to be nice to men like Isaac, just to get a bit of tea for us. I'd bring chests full of the stuff up from Bristol. She'd have as much as she wanted. I'd use a horse to pull my trow as well. There'd be no thieving bow haulers working for *me*.

I gave a last look at the trees along the river, now clear of mist and heavy with summery green. Then with a shudder, I turned back to the smoke and the choking smell of the pit bank. 'Bye, Maria,' I called, but she didn't hear me. She was climbing over the dusty heaps of coal on her way to do the sieving, and I felt Dad's hand suddenly grip my shoulder hard.

'Joshua, you take care of your mum and your sisters, whatever happens. You hear me?' he said, looking very stern.

I felt scared. He only called me Joshua when I'd been bad, or there was something important to say. I nodded, although I was frightened inside. Then he let go of me, his face creasing into a sort of twisted smile. 'There's Lloyd, so we'd best be moving,' he said abruptly. Then beckoning me to follow him, he joined the other men standing outside the engine house door.

Lloyd the banksman was strutting about shouting, 'Over here now, quick,' in his high squeaky voice as he flapped his plump hands in the air. He was a small man, wearing his best-striped waistcoat with a watch chain over his fat belly. Above his tasty neck cloth, his plump cheeks and nose were a reddish purple colour.

We gathered round him, waiting while he put ticks in his book against the names of the men and boys going down the pit that day. Dad said the banksman was too full of his own importance. That he spent long hours in *The Tumbling Sailor* supping ale and

19

men laughed at him behind his back. But Dad warned it was best to do as the banksman said, for he could put you out of work if he took against you.

Some of the men were already on their way towards the mineshaft. So when my name was called I hurried after them. The men were the first down in the wagons. They shoved us younger ones out of the way, cuffing us, but I always tried to push to the front of the queue. It was dangerous work, diving between the miners, holding onto my cannikin, and leaping into the wagon as it swayed over the deep hole. But it would mean an even worse beating from the horsekeeper if I were late.

Sometimes the men let me be, especially when Dad was near, but that morning I wasn't so lucky. A miner I hadn't seen before shouted, 'Get away, you little rat!' He grabbed me by my jacket so fierce that I tottered back, knocking down Billy Richards who was waiting his turn with the other kids in the queue.

'Sorry,' I said, pulling Billy to his feet. It wasn't hard to lift him, because there wasn't much of him. It was easy to recognise Billy under the dirt and tears making streaks in the coal dust stuck to his face. He was the smallest kid there, always hitching up his trousers that were too big for him.

On our one day off a week, Billy and me were supposed to go to Sunday school together. Billy hated going more than I did, so sometimes we ran off to play in the woods. Mum always knew. When I came home, my Sunday clothes were dirty. I expected a good thrashing, but mostly she didn't hit me. She just yelled a bit about ruining the only good clothes I had. Maybe she realised I needed to enjoy myself sometimes. I think that's why she didn't tell on me to Dad.

'What are you crying for Billy?' I said, when I'd set him back on his feet, but I knew the answer. He was more fearful of the mine than I was. He wanted to go home to his mum. I felt sorry for him. He was six. He'd been set to work at the pit sooner than me.

I tried to rub the coal dust off his face, but it just mixed with the tears, making him look worse. His mum didn't make him wash as much as our mum made me. He looked so funny with his big eyes staring out of the muck. I laughed and he stopped crying.

'Would you like to play with my best marble?' I said, fishing it out of my pocket. 'Here. You can't *keep* it, but I'll let you lend it for a day.'

His eyes got bigger when he saw the marble. I put it in his small fist and his fingers tightened round it. It was the best marble I'd ever had. There with no scratches on the smooth clay.

'You put it safe, now,' I warned him. 'Don't you go losing it, or you'll get a thumping.'

He cringed, looking like a whipped puppy. I wished I hadn't said I'd hit him, so I pulled faces at him till he started to giggle. Then I tickled him until he squealed, wriggling about like our Sara. I was trying to think of other ways to cheer him up when the banksman let out a bellow, making us jump.

'Hey! You two brats. You're last. Get a move on!'

Alarmed about being late, I hurried over to the top of the shaft. Taking Billy's hand, I pulled him towards the empty coal wagon. I was always afraid of the way it swung over the top of the hole, but I acted brave for Billy, trying to steady it as the men did.

It didn't matter how many times I went down the mine, terrible stories came into my head. Stories about the chain snapping, men falling to their deaths, or men crushed when the wagon came up so fast it crashed into the wheel at the top. Trying not to think about such things, I held tight to my cannikin with one hand and grabbed the chain with the other. Then I swung myself into the wagon, pulling Billy headfirst after me.

I sat down quickly to stop it rocking. Billy crouched beside me whimpering. He wouldn't shut up. I held tight to the chain, trying not to look over the side. There wasn't much room between the wagon and the wall of the shaft, but if the chain broke… it was best not to think about it.

'You'll be all right, Billy,' I said, but my heart was thumping with fear.

Billy clutched me tight round the neck nearly choking me. His tears mixed with the coal dust on his face and rubbed off on me. Then the bottom of the wagon fell away from us. We gasped, fell after it, and saw the sides of the shaft shooting by at a horrible speed.

3

Creaking and Groaning

My stomach fell separate from the rest of my body as we hurtled down the shaft. We were going so fast I thought we'd be smashed to pieces. I was desperate for the brake to go on in the engine house to stop us falling.

Billy was wailing and clinging to me. I was trying to shove him off when the wagon jerked to a fierce stop. It swung hard against the shaft walls, banging and tumbling us about. Moments later, we started to fall again but this time much slower. Then I felt a thump as the wagon landed hard on its iron wheels, and I sighed with relief for we were safe at the shaft bottom.

Trembling all over, I scrambled out, helping Billy after me. Standing in the huge underground cave that the miners had cut from clay and sandstone, I felt very small. Beyond the reddish glow from the braziers, the back of the cave was full of frightening shadows. I always imagined a huge animal was out there, crouched in one of the tunnels, waiting to grab me.

In the leaping firelight, I saw a pit bottom boy dart forward, unhook our wagon from the chain, and push it towards the others on a siding. The last men to come down the shaft were hanging their jackets and shirts on nails along the wall. Some were already hurrying towards the back of the cave, their boots crunching on lumps of coal and the light from their candles dancing wildly on the rough walls.

Knowing I was last down, and sure of another beating, I peered through the gloom towards the pit bottom stables built against the side of the cave. I was worried. There was no lantern hanging from the end stall. There was the smell of horse muck and dusty hay, but the place seemed deserted. Bradley the horsekeeper, the ponies, and the pony drivers were gone.

'Something's up,' I said to Billy.

I was trying to think what to do, when I felt long fingernails digging painfully into the back of my neck. I nearly left the floor with shock. Struggling to be free, I heard a deep sneering voice behind me saying, 'Having a look around? No work today? Thinking of going home, are we?'

I didn't need telling who had hold of me. I knew that voice. I'd felt that cruel grip many times before. With strong hands he twisted me round, forcing me to look up into his angry, pockmarked face. It was Isaac Whitlock, the pit bottom steward.

I hated and feared him. He was a bull of a man, towering over me. His barrel chest and broad shoulders gave him a look of strength that made other men wary of him. His white face was like bread dough, mostly hidden by a thick black beard that made him look creepy. He had wiry, grey-flecked hair tied back in a long greasy ponytail. It was his eyes, black and glittering in the firelight, that scared me the most. They reminded me of a snake.

His body smelled sickly sweet, like the soap he gave to Mum. He pushed his face closer to mine and I tried to turn my head away. 'Sorry, sorry Mr. Whitlock,' I muttered. My throat was dry with fear of the man. He was like the horsekeeper, quick with his fists.

I could hear poor Billy making bleating noises behind me. His small fingers were clutching the back of my jacket and I cried, 'The stables – what's happened to the ponies?'

'The ponies are gone to the old workings – where *you* should be. Serves you right for dawdling, you vermin. Get a move on – and take that whimpering brat with you – he's trapper on the first door. You'd best be quick if you don't want Bradley to skin you alive!' He laughed one of his long spiteful laughs. Then he gave me a push so hard I fell and Billy tumbled after me.

I scuttled away on my hands and knees, lumps of coal sticking painfully into me. Struggling to stand, I pulled Billy to his feet and hurried him towards the nearest brazier. Fumbling in my pocket for my candle, I'd scarce lit it when Isaac Whitlock let out an impatient bellow. Billy gave a terrified howl, throwing himself at me. I tried to shake him off, but he clung fiercely to my jacket, and as I hurried towards the back of the cave I dragged him along the horseway so fast his feet hardly touched the ground.

It wasn't until I'd almost reached the tunnel entrances that I realised, with a horrible sick fear, that I didn't know the way to the old workings. I was frantic. I daren't go back to ask. Trying to decide which way to go, I heard Isaac bellowing at me again, and I grabbed Billy's hand and bolted with him into the nearest passageway.

Splashing through dirty puddles, the glow from the braziers didn't reach us anymore, and the blackness of the tunnel thickened around us. In the faint light from my small candle it was hard to see much, and feeling for the plateway under my feet to guide me, I kept telling myself the dark couldn't hurt me.

I trudged on, all the time worrying if this tunnel was the right one, but the thought that we were going to the old workings, and that Dad would be there, comforted me a bit. Billy shuffled along beside me, with his trousers tripping him up, when suddenly he tried to make me let go of him and cried, 'Is this the way?'

'Course it is,' I said, giving him a shake. 'I've been this way many times. You'll be all right. Come on, will you.'

'Shan't,' he muttered and bit my hand.

'Ouch, that hurt! Stop it — if you don't I'll thump you,' I threatened, but he took no notice.

'Won't,' he sobbed. He kept struggling and shrieking that he wanted to go home. He dug his boots against the side of the plateway and refused to budge. I grabbed him by the back of his jacket, almost lifting him off the floor.

'I've warned you what I'd do to you if you didn't stop it,' I yelled, but whatever I said made no difference to him. He was too frightened to listen. He just kept trying to run away. Desperate to make him come with me, for the longer I stayed there the worse beating I'd get, I shouted, ' Billy, I'm going. You can stay here on your own in the dark if you want to. See if I care.'

He just whimpered more and more, so I said, 'All right, go back to Whitlock - tell him you're not working today.' Then giving him a shake that made him cry louder, I let go of him and marched off down the tunnel, leaving the darkness to swallow him up.

To my great relief, it didn't take long for my plan to work.

Soon I heard the sound of his small feet pattering after me. I didn't say anything. I was angry with him for making me later than ever and I just kept walking along the plateway. I could hear him stumbling behind me and snuffling, but he sounded so miserable that I stopped for him to catch up with me. Taking his hand again, I said gruffly, 'Don't worry, Billy, you'll be all right, we're nearly there.'

Although I told him that, the worry was growing stronger inside me. We'd been walking for what seemed a very long time. The tunnel went on and on forever. Billy kept saying his legs were tired and wanting to sit down for a rest, and the further we went, the more I was sure we were lost. Thoughts of walking for days, with us slowing starving to death, wouldn't go away.

With these dreadful fears running through my head, I tried to make Billy walk faster, but he was stumbling on the bottoms of his trousers and dragging his feet. Once, I thought I saw another tunnel off to the right and I pulled him towards it, but it was just a deep hole in the rock. I was almost crying with fear and disappointment.

It was deadly quiet down there, except for the crunch of our boots on the lumps of coal and Billy's snuffling. Sometimes a sharp creaking shattered the creepy silence and there were long groaning sighs. Each time it happened, Billy squealed in terror.

29

Clinging harder to my hand he whispered, 'What's that, Josh?'

'Don't be daft,' I said furiously. I was trying to be brave for both of us, but I could feel him trembling. He was frightening me out of my wits. 'You've heard that creaking lots of times before and nothing's happened, Billy. It's only the pit props holding up the roof. They sound scary when they creak and settle, but we're safe enough.'

'I dunna like it,' he muttered tearfully.

I tried not to listen to him. In the light from my flickering candle, I glanced nervously at the wooden posts on each side of the tunnel. Although I didn't tell Billy, those creaking sounds made me fearful. If the pit props and roof boards gave way, tons of soil and rock would crash down, smothering us.

He was muttering about people who'd died in the mine, about ghosts coming to get him. I couldn't stand it any longer and shouted, 'Shut up, you're lucky. Ghosts won't give you a beating like the one I'll get from Bradley.'

Another thing was scaring me. The deeper we went underground the more water dripped from the roof. It was trickling down the walls and almost over the horseway. I was desperately thinking I'd better turn round and take a beating from Whitlock, and I was shouting at Billy for splashing me, when I saw water lapping around heaps of rock scattered beside the plateway. Hardly daring to believe that I'd found the entrance to the old workings at last, I forgot my tiredness, and pulling Billy almost off his feet, I hurried forward to have a better look.

Beyond the piles of freshly hewn rock, there was a new looking branch line leading into another tunnel. I held up my candle, and cried, 'We're all right Billy. This must be where the men cleared the way to the old workings. We're not lost. We'll soon find your door!'

Following the plateway into the tunnel, it was only a short distance before we found it, a door of rough new wood. Feeling greatly relieved, I pushed it open, looking out for rats. Mostly they scuttled away when they heard you, but Dad said a sick one might fly at you if you took it by surprise.

On the other side of the door, the plateway looked rusty, as though there'd been no one along that stretch of rail for years, so perhaps the rats were gone. The roof of the old tunnel was lower, the walls narrower, and I didn't like it one bit. I tried not to, but I was thinking of the men and boys who'd died there. Billy kept going on about ghosts again, which made it worse. I snarled at him to shut up.

The roof was so low there was only just room for me to stand. I'd have to watch my head. The walls were glistening with wet. There were lots of puddles, but I was glad it didn't smell like our privy, as it did in the other tunnels. I closed the door behind us, shutting us in, and felt Billy twisting his fingers tight in my jacket.

'You stay here, Billy, this is your door,' I said as cheerfully as

 I could. 'I'll be back soon – you'll be all right. You sit where there are no puddles.'

I lowered my candle to show him a small dark hole cut into the wall, just above the plateway. He clung to me harder, making me feel awful about

leaving him. His mum couldn't afford to buy him a candle. When I left him, he would be alone in the dark. I found the bit of rope tied to a hook on the door. Wrapping it round his small fingers, I managed to be free of him.

'Hold on tight to that. Don't lose the rope or you won't find it again in the dark. Then you won't be able to let the drivers through your door. You'll be shouted at and thumped.'

'Dunna go, Josh,' he said, so quietly I could hardly hear him. Seeing him crouched in the hole made me feel bad.

'I have to, Billy, but I'll be back with Drummer. You'll have the other lads to talk to when they come through your door. You won't be that long on your own, I promise. I'll come for you when it's time to have a bite to eat.' I wondered if his mum had given him food or anything to drink. I thought I'd share what Mum had given me. Then I realised I'd left my cannikin in the wagon at the pit bottom cave and cursed my luck.

'You wunna forget me, Josh?' he whispered.

'Of course not, now you know what to do – you've worked as a trapper for a long time. You're an old hand, just like the men. Remember to keep your door closed till you hear the pony and wagons come along. Then let it shut after them when they're through.' I tried to think of something to say to cheer him up. 'You've the most important job in the mine, Billy. The men need you to keep the air going round the tunnels – so gas doesn't blow them to pieces. Don't you go sleeping and fall on the plateway or the wagons will run over you.'

'Will the rats get me?' he whispered.

'Of course they won't. They're more scared of you than you are of them.'

He started to whimper again, so I said desperately, 'Keep tight hold of that marble, don't lose it. Tomorrow we'll go down to the old clay pit. I'll learn you to swim. You'd like that wouldn't you?'

'Promise?' he begged.

I spat on my thumb. '*I wet my finger, I wipe it dry, I cut my throat, if I tell a lie.*' I held up my candle so he could see what I was doing and ran my thumb across my throat. He nodded and giggled and I left him holding onto the rope with one hand and clutching the marble in the other.

Splashing as fast as I could through the coal-blackened puddles along the roadway, I told myself I'd stay with him for a bit on my way back, even if it were more trouble for me. I was glad the young trapper on the next door didn't seem as fearful as poor Billy, but he wasn't in the dark. He had a bit of candle.

No one could take a pony from the stables without the horsekeeper's permission, so Bradley would be in a rage having to wait for me. The further I went the more desperate I felt. I was hoping I'd reach the stables before the last pony and its driver were gone to their day's work.

Stumbling over lumps of coal, the familiar smell of horse sweat and fresh dung, mixed with the sweet smell of new hay, drifted down the passageway towards me. Ahead of me, I saw a row of wooden stalls against the tunnel wall. With my heart thumping fearfully in my chest, I ran towards a certain beating.

4

A Stone by the Door

In the poor light from the lantern hanging on the end stall, I saw the horsekeeper. He turned his head quickly when he heard my footsteps and my heart sank, for all the ponies were gone.

Only Drummer, an old Welsh cob, was waiting. He set up a terrible din when he heard me. He stomped the ground, backing into the chain across the end of his stall, making it rattle. Letting out a sharp neigh, he noisily head-butted his wooden corn box. I was too busy trying to avoid Bradley's swinging fists to give the animal a welcome.

The horsekeeper caught me a blow that nearly knocked me to the floor. I staggered about till my head cleared a bit. The pain made me sick, but I didn't shout out. I knew better than to utter a sound. That would make him even madder. He'd take his belt with the large buckle to me.

'Get on with it,' he snarled. 'Keep me waiting will you, I'll learn you better!'

Trying to avoid his punches, I dived under the chain. Standing my candle on the rough wooden fencing of Drummer's stall, furthest from the straw, I reached for the pony's harness. I had to be quick. The animal was always eager to trap my fingers when I slipped the bit into his mouth, and it's not best done when you are frantic, with the horsekeeper standing over you.

Pushing the headpiece over Drummer's ears, I struggled to fasten his throat-lash, cheek-pieces, and lift his heavy collar down from the hook on the wall. He tried to swing round in his narrow stall, his teeth bared. The collar rubbed him sore and he hated it. I was used to him, knowing his ways. I had the collar and back-straps on, the pulling-chains slotted through the loops along his sides, before he had a chance to bite me.

My fingers were wet from water dripping from the roof. This made me slow with the buckle fastening and the horsekeeper madder still. I worked furiously, trying to keep hold of the slippery leathers. Drummer started a battle of wills with me the moment I was ready to back him into the horseway. Although he was old, he was still stronger and heavier than I was.

This time though, I was so desperate to get away from Bradley fear gave me strength. It didn't take long before I had the pony out of his stall. I gave a few jerks on his harness, shouting lots of *walk on*. He followed me reluctantly along the rails with his pulling chains dragging and rattling behind him.

I walked beside him, wondering how to get to the coalface,  my head hurting from the horsekeeper's clouts. I hadn't dared to ask the man. He might have flown into a fierce temper again. But it wasn't long before I found a passing place where two lines ran close together, and guessing it must be the way, I gave Drummer an encouraging pat, urging him on.

The pony was bad-tempered, but it wasn't his fault. We were both a lot alike. He suffered from sores on his back. I ached from the horsekeeper's beatings. At least I could go home at night, see the sky, and breathe the fresh air. He had to stay down here in the dark. I felt sorry for him, gave him another pat, and clouds of coal dust flew up from his coarse, dry coat, making me sneeze.

'I'm not staying down here for many more days,' I told the pony. He twitched his ears, listening to my voice. 'I'm going to run away, but I'm not leaving you down here. Maybe they *will* dig a canal from the river to the old workings, like Dad said. Then they won't need you no more, but I'm going to–'

Drummer had come to a sudden halt, jerking his head up and down and snorting. I tugged at his noseband, but he wouldn't budge. 'What's the matter, Drummer?' I cried and heard the faint sound of scraping shovels and the thump of picks, coming from some way down the tunnel. 'You've heard the sound of men working lots of times before. What's wrong, boy?'

Maybe he was in the old workings those many years before, when the explosion happened. I tried talking to him and tugged at his collar, but he braced his legs, rolled his eyes, and refused to walk on. He barged against me. I shouted at him, thinking he'd squashed the bread and cheese in my pocket, and suddenly remembered.

I said a silent thank you to Mum, for in the cloth with my food there *was* a carrot. I held it out in front of Drummer and he trotted forward, desperate to grab it from me. Keeping it just out of reach, I coaxed him along, and we hadn't gone far when I saw the glow of many candles ahead of us. Drummer whinnied, moved forward quickly, and taking me by surprise, nipped the carrot from my fingers.

Now busy with his chewing, he was happy to follow me into a small cave filled with flickering candlelight, where men were crouched beside the walls, or lying cramped in holes they had hacked with picks out of the narrow seam of coal. Water trickled

38

down onto them, making their naked skin wet and shiny, and the air was thick with coal dust. It was a terrible place to be.

The floor of the cave had several plateways crossing it. Another pony driver passed me on his way back to the pit bottom, his wagons loaded with coal. There was a line of empty wagons on a siding. Boys a little younger than me were shovelling great lumps of coal into them as fast as they could. I shuddered. I'd soon be old enough to do a man's work and take up the pick, and that made me more determined than ever to run away.

The miners had stuck their candles to the walls and floor, close to where they worked. In the dancing shadows, I saw a thin, scarred back and knew it was my dad. He was on his side in a hole, hacking at the seam just above his head. The coal was breaking in lumps and falling onto him. I think he noticed me, although he didn't say anything. He had wagons to fill and dared not stop.

I longed to speak with him, but I had to hurry. I knew I'd be in trouble if I didn't turn Drummer round quickly and fasten his pulling chains to the next line of wagons full of coal. There wasn't much room to turn the pony, but he was used to it from his years down the mine and made little fuss. Tucking his head obediently between his legs, he let me spin him round. I was thankful to him for not trying to bite me.

Then with his pulling chains fastened, I scooped up wet clay from the cave floor, stuck my candle to the first of his wagons, and cried, 'Walk on, come on lad, good lad, Drummer.'

He whinnied, curling his lip and squalling as the halter rubbed his back. His sores hurt him bad, but I kept pleading with him. Then after a while, he gave a loud squeal, used his tired old body to take up the weight of the wagons, and started to drag them along the plateway. Once the wheels were turning, and the pain of his back was less, he settled to his work, the coal wagons clattering and bumping the rails behind him.

He plodded at a steady pace, sometimes giving his harness a shake. It was a comfort to have the old, grumpy Welsh cob beside me. We had to stop once on a siding to let another pony and his driver pass with empty wagons. It wasn't till I was almost at the last door of the old workings that I remembered I'd left Billy sitting alone in the dark without a candle. I called out to him and heard a frightened voice say, 'Josh, is that you?'

He was where I'd left him, crouched in the small hole beside the plateway and I called to him again, saying, 'Yes, it's me Billy, are you all right?'

'Is it time to eat?'

I didn't want to tell him he'd only been there a short while, so

I said, 'Not yet, although it won't be long. I'll be through your door a couple more times. Then I'll stop and we'll have a bite to eat. Still got that marble safe?'

'Course,' he said. 'I wunna lose it, Josh.'

'Just think about it being Sunday tomorrow. I'll learn you how to swim.'

I stopped with him as long as I dared, but hearing a rattle of wagons on the plateway behind me, I grew worried the other lad would report me to Whitlock for holding him up. Telling Billy to open the door, I hurriedly led Drummer and his wagons through.

The return to the pit bottom cave didn't seem as far as when we came along it earlier, when I was thinking Billy and me were lost. There was another driver ahead of me. I could see the comforting glow of his candle, and it wasn't long before I was back at the cave, blinking and trying to get my eyes used to the light from the braziers.

The pit bottom boys ran towards me. Then unhooking Drummer's pulling chains from his wagons they pushed them towards the shaft while I looked nervously around for Isaac Whitlock. Thankfully, he wasn't about, so I took longer than I needed to attach Drummer's chains to the next row of empty wagons, sneaking a bit of rest for him and me. Then when I'd stayed as long as I dared, I patted Drummer, and after much

41

grumbling he set off again to the old workings to fetch another load of coal.

We'd been backwards and forwards several times that day. The first time I'd found Billy sleeping I'd cuffed him, but I didn't do it again. The next time I just gave him a shake. I'd had enough beatings from Bradley and I knew how it felt.

I think we were nearly half way through our twelve hours underground when it happened. I always knew the time by how tired and hungry I felt. I was on my way to fetch another load of coal, and Drummer was plodding along, his empty wagons clanking behind him. As I reached the entrance to the old workings, I shouted, 'Billy, it's me, open your door. Let Drummer through, it'll soon be time to eat.'

There was no answer. 'Wake up, Billy, open the door,' I cried. I listened for him shuffling about. I was angry with him for not saying anything. Thinking he'd gone to sleep again, I slowly realised something was different. I could see nothing, just darkness where the door should be. Stretching out my hand, I couldn't feel anything. Fearful now, I lifted up my candle. The door was wedged back with a stone.

'Billy, where are you?' I called, but still there was no answer.

I cursed, wondering if he'd wandered off to play with the trapper further down the tunnel. Now I was scared. The gas might be building up. I was angrily shouting his name when a sudden blast of air, thick with coal dust, stung my face and blew me off my feet. My candle was gone, there was a long rumbling noise, and I felt the ground shaking under me.

5

A Terrible Sight!

Lifted violently into the air by the explosion, I landed on my back with a thump. Icy water was soaking into my jacket, slopping up my sleeves. My eyes were full of coal dust and hurting. It didn't matter how much I rubbed them I couldn't see anything. I'd dropped my candle, the dark in a mine was thicker than the blackest night, and I didn't know where I was.

The sound of the explosion had come from the old workings. All I could think about was Dad and I was desperate to find out if he were safe. I heard Drummer shrieking, kicking the wagons, and trying to break free. His screaming made me frantic with worry. If he broke his legs, the horsekeeper would give me the worst beating of my life, put me out of work, and I'd have no money to give to Mum!

I could tell the pony was close by the noise he was making. Fearful he'd trample me, and not sure where I was, I felt the plateway pressing into my back, rolled over, and hit the tunnel wall. Dragging myself hurriedly to my feet, and keeping my boots against the edge of the rail, I shuffled nervously towards the awful din Drummer was making.

Terrified he'd knock me down and drag the wagons over me, I held out my hands to feel where he was. As I snatched at the air in front of me his head thumped me in the chest and I tottered back. Recovering from the shock of it, I lunged forward again and this time my fingers caught in his mane. I fought desperately to keep hold of him, but he reared up and lifted me off my feet. Smashing his hooves on the horseway, he flung me from him.

The wagons were clanking and rattling violently and sounding horribly close. I scrambled away from them on my hands and knees, my heart thumping. Grasping hold of crevices in the wall, I pulled myself back to my feet, terrified the maddened pony would kill me. I was shaking with fright but I had to stop him harming himself. I shuffled towards him again, holding out my hands and trying to touch him, when I suddenly realised I couldn't hear him anymore. His whinnying and kicking had stopped and for a horrible moment, I thought him dead. Then to my enormous relief there was the sound of him moving about again.

He must have heard the men running down the tunnel long

before I did. Candle light flickered on the roof and walls and when I could see, I was startled to find Drummer with his head close to mine, snuffing at my face. Miners carrying picks and shovels were squeezing with their backs against the wall, alongside his wagons, and pushing each other in their haste to reach the door to the old workings.

One man shoved me out of way shouting, 'Hurry and move the wagons, you idiot, we'll need room to bring out the injured. What are you waiting for?'

'I've lost my candle,' I cried. The miner cursed me, but he stopped long enough to give me a bit of lit candle. Then grabbing hold of Drummer's noseband, he tried to drag him further down the plateway, but the frightened pony bit him and the man punched him viciously on the jaw.

Miners crouching low were scurrying with bent backs through Billy's open door, and I saw the grim looks on their faces as they entered the tunnel. Clinging to my candle, my mind was full of fearful thoughts about Dad and I longed to follow them, but I couldn't leave Drummer.

I don't know how long I stood staring after them, watching until the light from their candles was gone. I think it was the noise of the pony, shaking his head and rattling his pulling chains that made me remember I had work to do. I took hold of his noseband, afraid he might start his rioting again, but the thump the miner gave him must have quietened him.

He let me unfasten his chains without a fuss, ducking his head and spinning quietly round. He didn't complain even as I fastened his chains to the other end of the wagons, and this made me feel anxious about him. He seemed bewildered, not like himself at all. Following me towards the pit bottom cave, he took the weight of the wagons on his poor back without squalling, plodding along with his head down.

'Sorry you were punched,' I said and the sound of my voice seemed to startle him. He twitched his ears, shook his head violently, and before I could stop him, set off along the plateway at an alarming rate.

'Whoa, Drummer. Whoa!' I shouted, but he took no notice of me. Now he was trotting so fast the wagons were shaking and I was afraid he'd topple them over. I clung to his collar and had to run to keep up with him. I tried to slow him down but he was too powerful. I was scared I'd fall and be crushed under the wheels and I yelled and yelled at him to stop.

I was thinking he'd pull my arms off, that I couldn't hold onto him much longer, when to my great relief he began to slow down again. His headlong charge turned into a steady plodding. He was panting, his heaving sides covered in sweat, and as the clattering of his wagons grew less I heard a very strange sound.

It was like a loud whispering, or the buzzing of angry bees, and it seemed to be creeping along the tunnel towards me. Drummer was listening too and moving cautiously forward, his ears twitching. We were close to the end of the tunnel as the loud whispering turned into a muffled roar. I was scared Drummer would bolt again, so I kept a firm hold on his harness, but I needn't have worried. Now I had to coax him forward, and as we entered the pit bottom cave the roar turned into a tremendous wave of noise that swept over and around us.

The pony brought the wagons to a violent juddering halt, and in the flickering glow from the braziers was a terrible sight. A line of wagons had toppled off the rails, trapping a maddened kicking pony beneath it. Drivers were shouting, trying to free it. The pit bottom boys were yelling, getting in the way, and running dangerously about. Small trappers were fighting each other, trying to be first to climb into an empty wagon at the bottom of the shaft, and I looked for Billy and couldn't see him.

Other lads were crouched on the floor, their arms over their heads. Ponies without drivers, wild with fear, were rearing up and dragging their pulling chains along the floor. Some had chains wrapped round their legs. One cob was frantically trying to break free. Drivers were yelling and running after their terrified animals.

Drummer backed his wagons along the rails, desperate to escape from the terrible noise. I clung to his collar, yelling to some pit bottom boys to help me. It took the strength of all of them to hold him while I freed him from his pulling chains and collar. Grabbing him by the noseband, I dragged him between

terrified ponies and overturned wagons, struggling to keep him from trampling the little lads who were screaming with fear and running around him.

'Where's Isaac Whitlock?' I shouted to one lad close by me as he fought to keep hold of his maddened Shetland.

'Don't know where he is,' he cried, panting with the effort of holding onto the pony, 'he's never here when there's trouble.'

There wasn't time to ask more. Drummer stretched out his neck, biting a pony on the rump, I was shouting at him to stop it, and I heard an angry bellow. Above the heads of the ponies and drivers around me, I saw one of the horsekeepers, and for the first time in my life, I was relieved to see him.

He was yelling at us to line up our ponies and follow him. The trappers, cowering at the bottom of the shaft, heard his voice and tried to run towards him. Pushing and hitting out with their small fists, they head butted their way through everyone, making the already terrified ponies rear and spin. I was struggling to keep hold of Drummer, trying to listen to what the horsekeeper was shouting, when somebody screamed, 'Fire!'

6

The Day of the Fair that Wasn't

There was a trickle of smoke drifting into the cave. It was coming from the tunnel that led to the old workings, bringing with it the smell of burning straw.

Thinking the old stables must be on fire, and fearful of another explosion, we dragged our animals after the horsekeeper. But he was leading us towards the back of the cave, where the smoke was thicker, and some of the drivers started to panic.

Turning round, they pulled their ponies into others behind them. In the terrible shouting, the tangle of pulling chains, and the crush of animals and drivers, I was sure we were going to die. Bits of burning straw floated over our heads. Trappers were running in circles and howling. Ponies without drivers were lashing out with their feet and bucking, their eyes rolling and their flanks heaving with fear.

We might have fought each other until the smoke grew so

thick we suffocated, but some of us noticed the horsekeeper disappearing into a tunnel, furthest away from the burning smell, with the little ones running after him, and this brought us to our senses. Our fear of staying there to die was stronger than our fear of the smoke, and we pulled our ponies after him. Those behind me pushed and shoved, wanting to be first into the tunnel. I clung fiercely to Drummer, swept along by the crush of the others around me, and felt my feet leave the floor.

Trapped in a heaving mass of ponies and drivers, the rump of one terrified animal was crushing me. I could hardly breathe. Another pony reared up, it hooves close to my head. I was losing hold of Drummer when a large barrel-sided pony charged forward. Now there was a small gap in front of me and I managed to get my feet back on the ground and could breathe again.

In the mad collision of yelling drivers and petrified ponies, those ahead of me surged forward, but the entrance to the tunnel was narrow, there was only room for one pony and driver at a time. Thumped by ponies on either side of him, Drummer swung round, biting a young cob on the neck. The younger pony battled to defend himself, but Drummer bit him again. Screaming, maddened, and terrified, the young cob tore free. Charging forward, frantic to escape, he scrambled over the backs of the

Shetlands in front of him and Drummer barged after him, pulling me violently into the tunnel.

In the flickering light of the horsekeeper's lantern, I saw a long line of ponies and drivers moving swiftly down the passageway ahead of me. Drummer lifted his feet, eager to follow them. I stumbled over the uneven floor, trying to keep up with him and surprised to find there was no plateway.

The pit bottom lads and trappers, frantic with fear, were pushing past us, getting in our way. They made it difficult for us to control our animals, and I was relieved when the passage widened a little. But my relief didn't last long, for soon the ground rose steeply and the ponies were struggling. Their hooves slipped on the rock-strewn floor, but with encouraging shouts and lots of pushing and pulling from the drivers, we managed to keep them moving. To my surprise, Drummer needed no encouragement. He seemed to know where he was going and charged nimbly up the slopes like a young colt, pulling me after him.

We were climbing for a very long time, my legs and back were aching, and I was wondering when we would ever reach the end of the tunnel. Even Drummer was beginning to show signs of tiredness and finding it hard to keep up with the younger ponies. I heard the horsekeeper shout that we were nearly there, but we needed no telling, for despite our exhaustion, we knew every step took us away from the explosion.

At last, the ground began to level out a little, the ponies panted less, and my legs felt less weary. It wasn't long before I began to feel cold air on my skin, there was a wonderful patch of daylight ahead, and we were at the end of our climb. The pit bottom boys and trappers whooped with excitement and ran ahead. Our ponies lost their tiredness and picking up their feet hurried after the little ones, trotting into the open air with tails and heads held high.

Stumbling out of the mine, I saw we were in an old stone quarry, the cliff face overgrown with stunted bushes. Foxgloves with long bell-covered stems were growing through crevices in the rock. Tiny holly bushes were pushing sideways out of the quarry walls and I tramped through knapweed and kidney vetch, the smell of the wild plants strong in my nostrils. Wading waist high in clumps of rose bay willow herb, grass seeds floated in the air around me.

It was so wonderful to be out of the mine. There was clear blue sky above me, the best I've ever seen, and I blinked in the sudden brightness, breathing in the clean air. Lads around me were shouting and yelling with relief, glad to be safe. I wanted to shout too, but I couldn't stop thinking about Dad, left behind in the old workings, and this took much of the joy out of me.

I'd passed this quarry many times, when I'd followed one of the paths from the pit bank through the woods to the river. But bushes hid the entrance to the tunnel and I'd never noticed it. Then I remembered Dad telling me about a place where they led the ponies into the mine for their first day's work and brought the sick and old ones out, and I muttered a thankfulness prayer I'd heard Mum say, for this tunnel had saved our lives.

We helped the horsekeeper to round up the loose ponies. The pit bottom lads and the small trappers had run off. It wasn't hard collecting the animals, for those without drivers huddled together and quietly followed us as we led our ponies out of the quarry and down the path through the trees to the river.

Not far from the riverbank, where men had cleared the land, there was rough pasture surrounded by stout wooden fencing. It was here the pit ponies, too old to work, were busily cropping the grass. I'd often visited them, thinking how lucky they were. They were free from the mine and not covered with sores like poor Drummer. They must have heard us, for they whinnied at our approach. Then with curiosity satisfied, they returned to their grazing.

Following the horsekeeper through the gate, we led our ponies into the field. They didn't move very far from us. They stood quietly, some tossing their heads, some with quivering skin as if flicking off flies. They seemed unwilling to leave us. We were anxious, wondering what was wrong, when the horsekeeper said, 'It'll take time till they're used to being outdoors again. They've been underground all their lives – they've forgotten what it's like. The daylight will hurt their eyes after years in the dark. Some will be so old they may be blind.'

This made me scared for Drummer, fearing he was blind too. I took a quick look at him. He seemed to be looking back at me. Now that I could see him in the daylight, I noticed where the coal grit had worked under his collar and pulling straps. His skin was rubbed off worse than I thought. Grit was stuck to the raw places.

I felt saddened to see his back bleeding and nasty looking. I patted him and told him how sorry I was for him. For once, he didn't push me away. I wondered how long he'd been underground, never being able to breathe fresh air or feel the sun on his back. I was glad for him to be there. He lifted his old head to sniff at me, and I was more determined than ever to take him with me when I ran away.

Then the horsekeeper called us, and we gathered round and we were shocked when he told us we could go home. We stood there, like our ponies, not knowing what to do. Going home before our workday ended was something that had never

56

happened before.

'Are the men in the old workings all right, Sir?' one lad said, daring to ask what we all wanted to know.

The horsekeeper shook his head. 'Don't know,' he said sharply. 'Be off home quick, the lot of you, before I change my mind.'

Giving Drummer one last pat, I hurried through the gate after the others. Once on the hill we started to run, racing each other up the path through the trees. We didn't stop until we reached the top of the pit bank and what we saw filled us with astonishment.

It was like a fair day. There were crowds of people, only they weren't wearing their Sunday best. It wasn't happy and noisy with the fairground organ clanging its cymbal and making jolly music as it did on fair days. There was a deathly hush, except for a few young ones whinging. It was mostly women from the cottages crowded close to the pithead shaft with a few old men.

People I didn't know must have come up from Coalport village, curious to find out what was happening, but they kept well away from us pit bank folk. There were so many people they were standing in huddles right up to the engine house and around the boiler shed.

It was horrible. They weren't saying anything, just standing there and waiting. The women from the cottages had their aprons on, as if they'd run from their homes in the middle of their work. Some jiggled wriggling babies on their hips. Others had little ones clinging to their skirts. Standing apart from the rest were the pit bank women and girls, all covered with coal dust like me, their frightened eyes staring from the muck.

I pushed my way through the crowds, climbing the slope till I was high enough to look down and see what was happening. I recognised the doctor's funny chimney pot hat above the heads of other men. He was standing close to the mineshaft with the vicar from Coalport and the mine manager.

Then the bell clanged, the winding engine thumped. The chain rattled and slithered over the pithead wheel and a mixture of hope and terrible fear was inside me. The men would be coming up from the mine at last. Afraid of the awful injuries I might see, I held my breath as the wagon rose slowly out of the ground. I dared hardly look. When I forced myself to do it, I saw two miners climbing out of the wagon. They didn't look hurt at all. The doctor and the mine manager hurried over to them and I was desperate to know what they were saying.

It wasn't long before the miners clambered back into the wagon, helping the doctor in after them. My fear grew stronger, not knowing what had happened. Worrying if Dad were safe, I watched helplessly as the wagon began to drop down the shaft.

The top of the doctor's hat was the last thing to disappear.

Then a buzz of talk from those nearest to the pithead grew louder and louder. News of what had happened was spreading through the crowd, passed quickly from one anxious group to another. I waited fearfully to hear what people were saying and saw Maria pushing through the crowds up the bank towards me. Her long hair had fallen from her hat in tangled strands. Her face was thick with coal dust, except for where tears had made streaks in the dirt.

From the way she looked, I was scared what she might say. But I had to know and I grabbed her arm and cried, 'Tell me! What's happened? Is Dad all right?'

She shook me off. 'The men are trapped in the old workings,' she said, muttering in a dead sort of voice. 'The explosion made the roof fall in – they're trying to dig them out – it'll take a long time to reach them.'

I stood there looking at her, feeling sick in my belly. Dad's words, about me looking after Mum and my sisters, were going round in my head.

'Where's Mum? Does she know?' I cried.

Maria pointed to Mum. She was in the crowd, standing close

to the pithead, holding Sara's hand.

'Does Mum know I'm all right?'

'I told Mum you were safe enough. I saw you coming up the bank.'

'What does *he* want?' I asked bitterly. I'd just seen Isaac pushing through the crowds towards Mum. 'I'm going to tell him to leave Mum alone!'

'Don't be a fool,' Maria said, clinging to my arm. 'You keep well away from him!'

I seethed inside. All I could do was wait on the bank, hoping Dad was all right. Hour after hour, we stood through that terrible afternoon. Some of the Coalport people drifted away as the sun sank slowly towards the ridge on the far side of the gorge. It was the longest day of my life. Babies started their tired, hungry, bawling. The fearful mothers were hushing them, the children at their feet crying and fretful too.

'Dad's all right, I *know* he is. He's not like that coward Isaac. Running away when there's danger, keeping safe on the pit bank,' I said fiercely, when I couldn't stand the quiet any longer.

Maria said nothing. She just kept looking at the ground. Then the bell in the engine house clanged, breaking into all our thoughts and making us jump. There was a murmur from the crowd. The wagon was on its way up the shaft again. In the sudden deeper hush, the wailing from the little ones sounded louder. Trying to be ready for what I might see, I heard a gasp from the people closest to the shaft.

The doctor was alone in the wagon, looking very strange with his face and tasty clothes covered in coal dust. He climbed out awkwardly and the mine manager hurried to speak to him. Soon we heard the grim news. There was little hope of digging the men out for days. Many women began to cry fearfully, the children to wail with their mothers, and my legs felt suddenly weak.

'That's not right,' I said to Maria, 'you'll see, they'll soon find a way to–'

Maria grabbed my arm. She was pointing to where Mum stood with Sara. Mum was swaying, about to fall, and Isaac put his arm about her, leading her slowly through the crowds.

'Keep your temper, Josh,' Maria warned. 'Best stay away for now – he's dangerous. I'll follow them and let you know when he's gone.'

She hurried away. I saw her catch up with Mum and Isaac, taking Sara's hand. I followed helplessly after them as they left the pit bank and walked along the road towards the cottages. I kept well back, but Dad's words about Isaac being bad, and about me looking after the family, wouldn't go away.

Isaac was almost at our door and I ran past him, stretching out my arms across the threshold to bar his way. Mum was holding onto his arm, swaying, white faced in front of me. She was looking at me without seeing.

'You can't come in, you've no right, it's Dad's house!' I shouted at Isaac. 'Go away – leave us alone – you're not wanted here!'

He was grinning at me in a terrible way. He strode forward, tearing me from the doorframe. I fell, hitting my head on the road. The pain was fierce and I heard Maria scream. Then the world went upside down and began to spin.

7

The Time for Running Away

When I opened my eyes, sunlight glittered through the tree branches above me. I was lying on the wooded bank behind our cottages, feeling dizzy and sick. A shadow moved across my face, making me flinch, but it was only Maria peering down at me, her eyes big and frightened.

'I thought he'd killed you,' she gasped.

'Where's Isaac?' I said, sitting up too quickly, making my head hurt more.

'Hush. You don't want him knowing where you are. When Isaac took Mum indoors, my friend helped me drag you up here. You're out of sight of the pit road, or anyone in the back gardens, but it won't be safe for you to stay long.'

'Dad?' I cried, hoping there'd be nothing to worry about, that it was just one of my nightmares. Maria didn't say a word. She turned her head away. From the look on her face, I knew the explosion had really happened.

'Mum?' I asked quickly.

'Shocked – she don't make any sense. Isaac's pretending to take care of her, fussing round her. She can't see how bad he is so she won't send him away. The doctor gave Mum something to make her sleep. When she'd gone to bed, Isaac sent me to look for you. He says he's going to whip some sense into you as soon as he finds you, and if you don't do as you're told, he says he'll send you to the workhouse.'

'He'll have to catch me first. Dad will be home soon. Then Mum will tell Isaac to go away!'

'Keep your voice down, Josh, there's nothing Mum can do. If something's happened to Dad, she'll need a man to pay rent for our cottage. Isaac has no place of his own. He lodges at Coalport, so he'll be keen to move in with us. Then he'll have Mum to look after him. He'll never budge. If Dad doesn't come back, Isaac will take your wage and mine. Sara's too, when she's set to work,' Maria said miserably.

'Well, he's not having *my* earnings,' I said, struggling to my feet. 'I'm leaving, but you must promise to take care of Mum and Sara till I come back.'

Maria looked very worried, but she slowly nodded. 'Where are you going, Josh?'

'Best you don't know, or Isaac will thrash it out of you. Perhaps it won't be for long.'

'I'll keep a look out for you. I'll creep out at night. If you–'

There was the sound of a cottage door opening. We looked at each other nervously. Isaac was shouting my name. We heard his boots crunching along the pit road.

'Quick, Maria, go back down,' I hissed at her. 'Tell Isaac you can't find me – keep him talking so I can get away.'

She looked at me in alarm. Then she disappeared silently into the trees. Not long after I heard her calling to Isaac and his answering shout. Fighting my dizziness, I climbed the hill as quickly as I could, keeping to where the trees were thickest.

A twig snapped under my foot and it sounded terrifyingly loud, making me jump. A startled crow flapped into the air with a harsh warning cry, making my skin crawl with fear. Expecting Isaac to come charging up the slope after me, I listened anxiously to every sound. Somewhere in the wood, squirrels bounced through rustling heaps of dried leaves and there was the slow buzz of flies, but I heard nothing more.

The silence of the wood felt eerie. I started to climb again, trying to ignore the pain in my head, and I didn't stop until I reached the last of the trees and came out onto the rocky, windswept ridge. Still scared Isaac might be searching for me I crouched close to an outcrop of limestone, looking nervously down into the valley on the far side of our hill.

Below me, sheep on stick legs balanced between scattered boulders, tearing noisily at the spiky grass with thin hard lips. On the valley floor, farmland spread out before me, criss-crossed  with roads, hedges, and dotted with hamlets and farmhouses. In the distance, high on a rise of land, I saw the tower of Kemberton church and the Severn flowing steadily between wide sloping banks with water meadows on either side.

Looking along the river, a movement caught my eye. Coming upstream towards Coalport was one of the bigger trows. I thought she was the *Victory.* I was sure I'd seen her leaving more than a week ago with a load of pig iron for Bristol. Watching the huge craft, I began to worry how I'd find work on her. Suddenly my idea of running away to sea didn't seem as easy as I thought it would be.

Another thing was troubling me. I'd be leaving Mum and my sisters with Isaac Whitlock, I didn't know what had happened to Dad, and all I truly wanted to do was to go home. I longed to start this terrible day again – to be safe home with Dad, Mum and my sisters. I'd have done anything to have that happen. I would even have taken Bradley's beatings forever if I could have had Dad back again.

But it was no use wishing. Isaac was probably looking for me along the Coalport Road, so I decided to go down the hill, through the fields, and take the long way to the village to avoid him. I started to scramble down the hill, but the track was so steep I slid, sending pebbles and small rocks bouncing ahead of me. Slithering dangerously past a startled sheep, I clutched at a boulder to stop myself falling.

Taking more care, I reached the bottom of the hill, breathless, with my legs trembling, and started to walk across the fields. Tramping through ripening barley towards a distant hedge, I found a few blackberries. Hurriedly cramming them into my mouth, I suddenly remembered I'd had nothing to eat since my porridge at breakfast. Feeling in my pocket, I pulled out the bread and cheese Mum had given me, eating it as I walked along.

There was a stream gurgling in the ditch close by. Splashing my face, I scooped up some water in my cupped hands. I was taking a long drink when I noticed the sun was close to the top of the hill, on the far side of the valley. If I didn't hurry I might reach Coalport too late to ask for work, and alarmed, I scrambled through a hole in the hedge and set off as fast as I could down the lane.

It was a long walk to the village, but I ran some of the way, stopping now and again to get my breath. Coming to the end of the fields, where the lane led onto the Coalport Road beside the river, I took a quick look along it. I wanted to make sure Isaac wasn't anywhere about, but there was no sign of him. Still glancing behind me from time to time, I hurried along the road towards the bridge leading into the village.

Crossing the bridge, I reached the first of the cottages that stood well back from the river along the cobbled street. Opposite the cottages were factories, forges, the new pottery with its bottle kiln, and the large brick warehouses crowded together on the riverbank. High above the warehouse roofs, netted boxes and barrels were swinging dangerously from cranes on the quayside, and I was relieved to see there was still time to ask for work.

As I walked quickly along the street, I heard coal rattling down the chutes into waiting barges, carters shouting and cursing as their horses struggled with heavy loads. There were whistles and shouts from the watermen busy on the quay. Surrounded by all this noise, and so many people moving on the street and in the alleyways, I felt much safer.

Passing the cottages and alehouses, I saw the tops of masts high above the warehouses and felt suddenly excited. The trows were close by. Anxious to ask for work, I ran towards an alleyway that led to the quay, and I was weaving in and out of the crowds when I saw Isaac.

He was in front of me, walking swiftly towards *The Tumbling Sailor*, an inn halfway down the quay, and sometimes stopping for a moment to look around him. Terrified, I turned, shoving people out of my way in my anxiety to escape, and ignoring their angry shouts I started to run back towards bridge.

But the Coalport Road was almost deserted, and if Isaac was following me, he would see me easily. Noticing a lane on my right I darted into it and found myself running along the backs of the long narrow gardens and workshops belonging to the cottages that faced the quay. Seeing low passageways under some of the first floors of the cottages, separating each one from its neighbour and leading onto the waterfront, this gave me an idea.

If I crept down one of the passages towards the quay, I might be able watch who was on the street, and keep a look out for Isaac. Finding a low fence, I scrambled over it into the nearest garden. Then jumping over rows of cabbages, I was running down a path towards the passageway, when I heard a dull thumping. Realising the noise was coming from the open door of the workshop in front of me, I tried to turn back, but it was too

69

late.

A man at a workbench, chopping meat with a cleaver, looked up and saw me. We stared at each other for a moment. Then he recovered from his surprise and vaulted over the bench. Yelling at the top of his voice, he ran at me with the cleaver.

I backed away, slipped off the edge of the path, and fell into bushes. Scrambling frantically to my feet, and too terrified to look where I was going, I ran straight into a wall. Hearing the man close behind me, I leapt at the crumbling brickwork, scrabbled frantically to the top of it, and threw myself over.

Crashing onto a pile of wooden barrels on the other side, I felt them wobbling under me. Clinging to the wall, I pulled myself to my feet and hopped frantically from barrel to barrel, trying to keep my balance. Below me was a cobbled yard, it looked a long way down, but hearing threatening shouts from the man with the cleaver, I jumped.

Painfully jarring my back and knees, I'd landed in the side yard of *The Tumbling Sailor*. A high wall surrounded it and there was a stable block built close to heavy wooden gates. Guessing that was the way onto the quay, I fled across the cobbles. I was tugging at the heavy gate bolts when I heard the sound of a door opening. Looking around in terror, I saw there was a side entrance from the inn into the yard that I hadn't noticed.

I wouldn't be able to open the gates before someone saw me, and I ran towards the stables, looking for a place to hide, but there was a dray loaded with barrels blocking the doorway. Putting my foot on top of one of the wagon's large wheels, I grasped hold of the narrow rail on the side of the cart, pulling myself up. Climbing onto the rail, I walked along it, swaying dangerously, and tried to squeeze between the top of the barrels and the doorframe, but there wasn't room.

Hearing angry voices, I snatched at the stable roof and hauled myself onto it. Managing to get one knee on the edge of the slates, and then the other, I began to climb, but I didn't get far. Some of the slates were missing. Frightened I'd fall through into the stables below, and clinging to the battens, I flattened myself against the roof. With rusty nails sticking painfully into me, I looked fearfully down into the yard and saw Isaac.

If he lifted his head, he would be sure to see me. I lay as still as I could, hardly breathing, and tried to stop my body from trembling. But for once, luck was with me. Isaac was arguing with Lloyd the banksman and he didn't look up.

Beside them was a small, thin man in a leather apron who kept nodding and looking nervous. I thought he must be the innkeeper. I didn't recognise a fourth man, standing a bit away from the others and listening to the argument. He was as tall as

71

Isaac was and had the face of a hawk. His hooked nose and hooded eyes made him look sinister and powerful. He wasn't dressed like a waterman. He wore fine woollen breeches, a jacket with many buttons, polished riding boots that came to the knee, and carried a whip in one strong looking fist.

To my horror, the men were walking slowly towards the stables, Isaac doing all the shouting. My body shook so much with fear that I was afraid my trembling would make the slates rattle and give me away. I cringed, expecting at any moment the men would notice me, but they suddenly disappeared from view.

For a joyful moment, I thought they had left the yard, and thinking I now had a chance to escape, I was about to move when I nearly jumped out of my skin. I could hear them talking just below me. They must have been standing close to the stable wall. If I reached down they were probably close enough to touch, and I could hear every word.

'I told you – we've got to move the rest of the goods out of the warehouse tonight,' Isaac growled.

'We can't do anything now, it's too dangerous.' It was the squeaky voice of Lloyd the banksman. 'Best wait till–'

'*Wait!* It's too dangerous to wait, you idiot,' Isaac snarled. 'There'll be no work at the mine for a couple of days – so now is our chance to do it. The longer we leave the stuff where it is, the more risk of it being found.'

It went quiet for a bit, then I heard a thin nervous voice say, 'I don't think–'

'Who asked you to think?' Isaac threatened. 'Just make sure that dray of yours is ready, so the stuff can be moved to Wenlock at first light, or I'll–'

'Less of that!'

A strong voice I'd never heard before rang out, making me flinch. It sounded like a voice used to giving orders, a voice that expected obedience without question. I guessed it was the fourth man with the brooding face of a bird of prey. 'Let the innkeeper be, Whitlock,' he growled. 'He'll be no use to you if you beat him senseless. Let him go. I'll see he keeps to our agreement.'

'You'd best make sure he does,' Isaac said fiercely, though he didn't sound quite as threatening as he usually did. 'And just you stick to *your* side of the bargain, see.'

'I'll be in Wenlock before nightfall,' the other said scornfully, 'keep your temper – you'll get your money.'

'I'd better,' Isaac said. 'Did you bring the key to the warehouse?'

After a moment or two, I heard footsteps on the cobbles again. I waited, thinking the men had left the yard. Then anxious to make sure, I lifted my head, lost my grip on the battens, and

73

started to slide down the slates. Unable to stop, I flew off the edge of the roof and landed with a thud at Isaac's feet.

Recovering my balance, I looked up at him in horror. The astonishment on his face was turning rapidly to black anger. His snake eyes were tiny points of madness in his head. He lunged at me and I jumped back, knocked into the banksman, and sprinted for the gates. Putting one foot on an iron bracket, I snatched at the top of the wooden doors. Hauling myself up, I felt Isaac grab my boot. Kicking wildly with my other foot, I heard him give a yell and felt him let go of me.

Dragging myself over the top of the gates, badly hurting my ribs, I dropped down into the road. Not knowing which way to go, I pushed frantically through the crowds. Finding a narrow alleyway between the warehouses, I fled down it and ran onto the quay. Charging head down through the watermen, I heard a commotion behind me. Glancing back, I saw Isaac pushing people violently out of the way and shouting, 'Stop him! Stop that thief!'

Leaping over boxes, I knocked into some barrels and sent them rolling over the cobbles. Ducking under the outstretched arms of a waterman who tried to grab me, I collided painfully with a pile of logs. Noticing a gap in the timber, I crawled frantically into it until I could go no further, and lay there, panting and fearful Isaac would find me.

Curling up tight and making myself as small as I could, I felt the logs moving under me. Terrified they would slip and crush me, I wriggled frantically backwards. Desperate to escape from my hiding place, I reached the end of the logs, felt about for the cobbled quay with my foot, but there was nothing under my boot.

Alarmed, I twisted painfully round in the narrow space. Peering out over the edge of the timber, I saw the ground rapidly disappearing beneath me. Leaning out as far as I dared, and turning my head to look up, I saw a large iron hook. The swaying logs were attached to the arm of a crane and rising higher and higher into the air. Isaac was standing on the quay, staring up at me. His head was back, his mouth wide open, and he was angrily waving his fist.

He ran towards the man operating the crane and yelled something and I felt the logs jerk up and down. Then they swung violently round and round, making me giddy. Unable to hold on, I was flung from the timber and tumbled through the air. Narrowly missing the quay, I landed with a splash in the river.

8
Sam

Icy water closed over my head. Weighed down by my boots and heavy work clothes I sank like a stone. The wooden sides of a vessel rushed past me in a mass of bubbles. Frightened the thick forest of reeds on the riverbed would tangle round my legs I lifted my arms, kicked frantically, and rose to the surface in a huge gush of river water, gasping for breath.

For one horrible moment, I couldn't tell where I was. Staring into the heavy gloom, I slowly realised I'd fallen between the steep sloping side of a trow and the wall of the quay. Trapped in a narrow strip of water, there was hardly room to move and little sunlight reached me. The river rose and fell powerfully, threatening to suck me down under the hull. I grasped at the wall, my fingers slipping on the wet blocks of stone.

The hawsers creaked as the heavy vessel swayed and dipped at her moorings. Terrified she might swing against the quay and crush me, I pulled myself slowly along towards her stern. The trow dipped with every movement of the Severn, making the freezing water slop against my head. Fighting to cling to the wall, my fingers growing numb with cold, I was horrified to hear someone walking on the cobbles above me.

I stayed as still as I could. The footsteps stopped just above my head. Looking up I saw a man's boots and the bottoms of his trousers. He was standing on the quayside, blocking out most of the light filtering down into my watery prison, and I was fearful it was Isaac. The strength in my numbed fingers was growing less. The river gurgled round me. In the misery of my wet dark hole, the bitter cold seeped into my bones. Struggling to keep my head above water, I was beginning to feel strangely sleepy.

It was such a comfortable drowsy feeling that I let it take hold of me, and I made no more effort to fight the pull of the river. My fingers slid down the wall, water rose over my chin. I was happily welcoming sleep when I heard Dad say sternly, 'Joshua, take care of your Mum and your sisters,' and felt his hand gripping my shoulder.

Suddenly alarmed at what was I was doing, I fought against

this dangerous lulling feeling. Spitting out river water, I saw pale sunlight filtering down between the hull and the wall. Whoever had been standing on the quay above was gone.

Battling against the river swilling around me, I dragged myself along the curving stern of the vessel. I had to escape from under the hull. Slowing and painfully I moved towards the massive rudder. I could see it sticking above the water, most of it a dark shape below me. Fearfully letting go of the wall, and fighting the sodden weight of my clothes, I kicked wildly, flinging my arms out towards it.

Grasping the thick outer edge, my fingers slipped on the wet wood. I snatched at the rudder again, and this time I managed to hold on. Pulling myself slowly to the other side of this huge piece of solid timber into open water, and half-swimming and half tearing at the hull with frozen fingers, I worked my way round her stern to her weather side.

Hidden from the quay, I clung to the rough tarry caulking between the trow's wooden planks, wondering how much longer I'd be able to hold on, and looked across the Severn to the opposite bank. At first, I thought I might swim across, but the river current was too fierce and I had little strength left. But if I didn't get out of the river soon, it would be the end of me.

Desperately trying to keep a hold of the caulking, something

78

hard whacked me against the side of my head, and I lost my grip on the hull. My fingers slid down the side of the vessel. I clawed frantically, tearing at the wood with my nails, found a gap between two planks and held on grimly, trembling with shock.

Exhausted, I craned my neck, expecting to see Isaac Whitlock looking down at me, but all I could see was the curving side of the trow towering above me. Moments later I heard someone shout, 'Quick, grab hold.'

A thick rope slithered down the side of the hull towards me. It was swinging and bouncing. I tried to catch hold of it, but the knotted end slipped through my cold useless fingers. Cursing helplessly, I heard encouraging shouts, and tried again. This time, when the rope came near me, I managed to catch hold and hang on. Hauled spinning and bumping against the side of the trow, I rose rapidly through the air. Dragged over the gunnel, I landed with a thump on the stern decking.

Lying in a bruised and sodden heap, I saw a broad face with bright gingery-brown eyes and an enormous wide grin looking down at me. Then a work-hardened hand, as wide as a shovel, pulled me roughly and effortlessly to my feet. Slapped on the back in a hearty welcome by my rescuer, I was almost knocked to my knees.

It was a waterman, wearing a torn red neckerchief knotted in the neck of his collarless shirt under an old jacket, and a faded yellow waistcoat covered his wide chest. He was a cheerful sight. Tufts of curly carrot-coloured hair straggled from under a wide brimmed floppy hat that was too big for him. His large ears seemed to be keeping it in place. He had pale skin with red weathered patches, and ginger freckles as big as shillings. His large broad nose was freckled the most. He was about the same height as me, but he wasn't skinny like I was, he'd filled out more. I thought him probably the same age as our Maria.

'Saw you being chased,' he said. Then he must have noticed me looking nervously along the quay for he said quickly, 'You dunna need to worry – the bloke chasing you – he went to the inn. He told someone to keep an eye out for you.' He held out his hand again. 'Name's Sam.'

'Joshua,' I said, 'but people call me Josh.'

He was looking down at the dirty puddles I was making on the scrubbed deck. Removing his hat, he scratched his mop of red hair. 'Best clean you up, or I'll have the maister after me when he sees that mess. Seem to have brought half the mine with you. Dunna want you getting your death, neither. Just you wait here.'

He stuffed his hat back on his head. Wedging it firm against his ears, he clattered down the short ladder into the hold. I heard him rummaging around below deck. There was a clanking noise. Then he came back carrying a bucket, bits of sacking, and a bar of rough-looking soap like Mum made at home.

Leaning awkwardly over the gunnel, he let down the bucket. Bringing it up, river water slopping over the brim, he put it at my feet. I kicked off my boots and the rest of my soaked things. He poured the icy water over my head, but I was so cold already I couldn't feel it. Then he gave me a bit of rough sacking, and I smeared it with soap. I scrubbed hard at my body till I was red with the rubbing and most of the coal dust had gone.

He handed me more sacking. I dried myself as best I could, giving my hair a fierce rubbing, and he disappeared down the ladder again. This time he returned with a pair of old canvas trousers, a worn out shirt, a jumper full of holes, and some woollen stockings that looked far too big for me. But it felt good to be rid of my dirty clothes and be free of the coal dust. My skin tingled after the bitter cold of the river, and I glowed all over as I struggled into the clothes he'd brought me.

'You'll do,' he said, after he'd carefully inspected me. Then nodding with satisfaction, he swilled the coal dust from the deck and told me to follow him.

Hastily turning up the bottoms of my borrowed trousers, I hitched up the sleeves of the jumper. Picking up my wet clothes,

I tucked my boots under my arm and climbed down the ladder into the empty hold. Taking care not to trip over the ends of the stockings that flapped as I walked, I followed him to a cabin, tucked under the aft decking. Holding the door open, he said with an enormously pleased grin, 'You'll soon warm up in here.'

The cabin was small but cosy and warm inside. On one wall was a coat hanging from a wooden peg and beneath it a pair of boots. Sam took off his hat and hung it beside the coat. There was a bunk bed built against the hull. Opposite were a small table and two chairs.

'Is that where you sleep?' I asked, pointing to the bunk bed. I felt envious, for the blanket and pillow looked comfortable. Not like our sacks filled with straw and old blankets at home.

He chuckled. 'Nah - that's where the maister sleeps. I'm only the second mate. Me an' Griffiths – he's the first mate – it's the store room under the foredeck with the spare sails for the likes of me an' him.'

Beyond the bed, part hidden by a bulkhead, was a small kitchen with an iron stove, cupboards, and a table covered with an oiled cloth. The heat from the stove filled the cabin and I was glad of it. The warmth I'd felt after coming out of the river was gone.

'You hungry?' he said. Not waiting for a reply, he squeezed

into the kitchen, beckoning me to follow. There was only room enough with us squashed up together. It was difficult to turn round without knocking into things. He took my boots from me, put them to dry next to the stove, and hung my wet clothes on a rail.

Struggling to take a pan and a spoon from one of the small cupboards, he dodged the drips from my wet trousers. Then clumsily scraping lumps of leftover potato and a few bacon scraps from a plate, he dropped them into a pan on top of the stove. Some of the food fell on the floor, but he just scooped it up with the spoon and tipped it back in the pan.

Stirring vigorously, he dipped his finger in the mixture from time to time to make sure it was hot enough. Then satisfied, he spooned out the food, moving bits from one plate to another to make sure we had the same. Adding a chunk of dry bread to each plate he handed me mine, grinning at me in a kindly way. Waving a hand towards one of the chairs, he gave me what seemed to be the only spoon.

Nodding at me, and then at the food on my plate, he sat down beside me saying, 'Eat up.'

Despite my weariness, and having eaten Mum's bread and cheese, the smell of the bacon made me ravenous. I chased the bacon and potato round my plate with the spoon and he scooped up his food with his fingers.

Watching him cramming potato into his mouth, I suddenly remembered he'd saved my life and I'd never given him a word of thanks. Feeling suddenly ashamed of myself I said, 'You must think me an ungrateful wretch. Not thanking you for pulling me from the river.'

He muttered something with his mouth full. It sounded like *I did now't* and *dunna mention it*. Then gulping down the last of his bacon and potato, he wiped his mouth on his sleeve.

When the meal was over, he busied himself in the tiny kitchen, tipping tea leaves into two mugs and adding boiling water. Then he invited me to sit on the bunk beside him. I wrapped my hands round my mug of tea, feeling the liquid warming me inside and out. Leaning my back against the bulkhead, and listening to the comforting sound of the kettle hissing gently on the stove, I thought for a moment of home and stared at the floor, wondering if I would ever be able to return.

Sam must have noticed, for he said, 'Cheer up, Josh, it can't be that bad.' Then after a bit, when I didn't say anything, he said, 'That bloke who was chasing you – I heard him shouting – had you stole something?'

'No,' I said with sudden anger. 'I don't steal. I came to Coalport to find work.'

'All right, all right,' Sam said with a gruff laugh, 'dunna get all worked up. The men round here can be a bit fiery – turn nasty at times, especially with the drink in 'em. An' people take none too kindly to those from the pit bank.' Then he looked uncomfortable. His face reddened under his freckles, and he added quickly, 'You being covered in coal dust, see.'

He hurriedly went back to drinking his tea, slurping it like Mum always told us not to. Then he said, 'Hope you dunna mind me asking, but seems odd somehow. I heard as how the pay's better in the pit, even for kids like you.'

'Kid yourself. I'm twelve,' I said, telling a lie and trying to guess how old he must be. 'I'm old enough.'

'No offence,' he said looking at me in his friendly way. Then he thought for a bit and said, 'Heard there was an explosion at the mine?'

He didn't wait for an answer. He just busied himself in the kitchen, putting our dirty plates in a bowl and pouring water over them. Then he came back, filling my mug with more tea, though I didn't ask. His kindness to me was so comforting that all my worries about Dad burst out of me and I cried, 'My dad's trapped in the mine!'

Sam jumped, slopping his tea, and staring at me. Once I'd started to tell him things, I couldn't stop. It was such a relief to be able to tell someone. I told him about Billy. How the tunnel roof had collapsed and miners were trying to dig the men out but it was going to take a long time. Then when I'd finished, and was out of breath with the telling, Sam gave a long low whistle.

'The explosion – I heard it, seemed to shake the quay it were so fierce.' He was frowning heavily at the thought of it and his freckles joined across his forehead. He ran his fingers through his shock of red hair.

'I can't go home,' I said miserably. 'Isaac will beat me when he finds me. He says he'll send me to the workhouse. If he doesn't kill me first! But I don't want to leave Mum and my sisters with no one to look after them. I promised Dad I'd care for them if something happened to him....'

Sam nodded, making clucking noises with his tongue. He scratched his head. 'What's to be done?' he said.

'Worse still, just now I was in the yard of *The Tumbling Sailor*. I overheard Isaac talking to some men about robbing the warehouse. He saw me, gave chase, and I fell in the river. He won't give up till he finds me, or is sure I drowned in the Severn. He'll think I'll tell on him.'

Sam gave another low whistle. 'There's been lots of thieving of late. The bow haulers have always stolen from the trows, but there's been more stuff disappearing from the warehouses – an' bigger things too, not just jugs of cider.'

'It's Isaac,' I said, grimly. 'I heard him talking to someone. I think it was the innkeeper. Lloyd the banksman was with him. There was another man, I don't know who he was, but I know for certain if Isaac catches me, he'll make sure I can never tell anyone what he's up to.'

'No, he wunna do that. Not if I can stop him!' Sam said fiercely, his eyes glittering. 'Who's Isaac?'

'He's pit bottom steward at the mine. Dad says he killed a lad who was going to tell about his stealing. I thought if I found work on the trows, I'd be safe from him. Maybe earn enough to come back and give money to Mum. Then she wouldn't need Isaac to buy food or pay the rent, if something bad has happened to Dad.'

'I can ask the maister,' Sam said thoughtfully, 'but I dunna hold much hope. He's stingy with money – would rather work me an' the mate till we drop – we're always shorthanded. I think he'd get rid of me if he could, if he could manage without me.' He frowned and his freckles joined together again. 'He's always blaming me for things when it's not my fault. I have to be careful, dunna want to be turned off.'

'Won't you be in trouble when he comes back and finds me here?'

'Nah – he wunna be back for ages. Let me worry about that.'

It was a relief to have Sam there, to share my worries with him. I began to feel a bit better and was imagining how it must have been for Dad when working as a waterman. 'Sam,' I said, 'how did you come to work on a trow?'

'I didn't have no choice. My Mum died when I was born. Dunna know who my dad was. I had no one to look after me, so it was the workhouse orphanage for me. I was beaten a lot – ran away often – but they always found me an' brought me back. Then I was 'prenticed to Yates an' I've been here since. He's not that bad to work for, 'cept when he's the worse for drink. Then if you have sense, you keep out of his way. I've been 'prenticed to him as long as I can remember. Not sure how long that is, dunna know how old I am. Think I must be fourteen, maybe older.'

'Yates must be very rich, having a trow like this,' I said.

'He dunna *own* the *Emily*.' Sam laughed long and loud. 'Though you'd think he owned her – the way he lords it over everyone. You should see him, strutting about like one of the gentry. Thinks he owns all of Coalport.'

My mouth fell open. 'What did you say?' I cried. 'The *Emily*? Is this the *Emily Grey*?'

9

Sam has an Idea

Sam nodded. 'Yes, you're aboard the dear old *Emily.*'

'Dad sailed on this trow,' I cried excitedly. I looked round the cabin, at the beautiful elm planking, the bunk bed, and the warm kitchen, as if seeing it for the very first time.

I could hardly believe I was on board Dad's lovely old trow at last. I'd day dreamed about this since I was small, listening to Dad telling me about his adventures. Now that I was really aboard her, I imagined Dad walking into the cabin and giving me a hug. For a moment, the thought filled me with warm happiness.

'Dad sailed on the *Emily* as first mate – maybe even ate off the plate you gave me,' I said. Sam pretended not to notice as I quickly brushed away a tear. 'It's because of Dad that I've always wanted to work on the *Emily*.'

'I wouldna be on any other trow,' Sam said. He sounded very proud. 'I love living on her, even with the beatings Yates gives me. There's no finer trow on the Severn, or anywhere else in the world. It's a good life, an' the beatings are less now I'm bigger and he finds me useful to have around. Especially when he an' the first mate have had a belly full of ale an' must sail the next day for Worcester.' He winked at me. 'Yes, they need me *then* all right.'

'Tell me about the *Emily*,' I begged.

Sam looked pleased and his eyes shone. 'She's had some adventures has this old lady, but she's still as good as the day she were built. Nearly sunk twice. The first time the bow haulers tangled the towing lines an' she drifted into Worcester Bridge. Nearly drowned the maister,' he said with a wicked chuckle. 'She was out of action for a long time after that, though that was before my time. Then someone saw her at Stourport, repaired her, an' brought the old lady back to life. That's when Yates took over an' I was 'prenticed.'

Listening to Sam's stories made me long to have adventures and sail down the Severn to Bristol. I wanted to see Worcester, and the other places on the river Dad told me about. It seemed such a wonderful life. Sam was telling me a long story about

90

riots at Worcester port. I listened, but the warmth of the stove, and the sound of the Severn slapping against the hull, must have lulled me to sleep. Waking with a start I heard someone shout, 'Sam, where are you?'

Sam frowned at me, putting a warning finger to his lips. 'Stay here an' keep quiet, it's the maister, he's back early,' he whispered.

I heard a voice I thought I recognised shouting, 'Sam. Come here, where are you?'

He slid off the bunk, cramming his hat onto his head. Hurrying out of the cabin, he quickly closed the door behind him. I looked around for somewhere to hide. If I were caught on board, I knew there'd be trouble for me *and* Sam. Noticing a small cupboard under the bunk, I fell on my knees and opened it.

It was full of blankets and a jumble of clothes. Cramming them together, I managed to crawl in beside them. It was such a tight squeeze I couldn't close the cupboard after me. I shuffled frantically about, banging my head. Pulling my knees up under my chin, I curled up tight, shuffled about a bit more and managed to shut the door.

Lying cramped in the dark, I waited anxiously, listening to the gurgling of the bilge and the smack of the river against the hull. Squashed up against old clothes and scratchy blankets, with their sour smell of sweat choking me, I heard heavy boots thumping across the cabin floor.

The footsteps were coming towards the bunk and I cringed as close as I could get to the back of the cupboard. Thinking the slightest movement I made would give me away, the door of my hiding place was flung open and I saw Sam's upside down head peering in at me.

'What are you doing in there?' he chuckled. 'It's all right. Yates is gone an' the first mate is over at Jackfield where his missus lives. He wunna be back till morning.'

He helped me out of the cupboard. He looked pleased with himself, tipping his hat onto the back of his head. He stuck his thumbs in the pockets of his faded yellow waistcoat, as I'd seen the watermen do. 'Told him I was in here, cleaning up, an' luckily he was in a hurry to be off. You're safe for a bit,' he said cheerfully. 'When he comes back, he'll have the bow haulers to pay an' he'll be drinking in the *Sailor* for hours. He'll be drunk, so it'll be safe for you stay on board till morning – you can sleep in the storeroom if you like.'

'What will he do when he finds out we've eaten his food?' I asked, but Sam just laughed. 'I'll tell him a rat ate his dinner,' he said and winked at me. Then he busied himself in the kitchen, refilling our mugs with strong, dark tea. We settled on the bunk again, and after a while he said, 'What are you going to do if Yates dunna take you on?'

'I'm scared Isaac will find me if I stay around Coalport long – I need to get as far from here as I can. If I walk to Wenlock, maybe I'll find work on a farm. But it's hard to leave without knowing if Dad is safe. I'm worrying about my mum, my sisters too. I told Dad I'd look after them if anything bad happened.'

Sam looked very serious, then after a while he said, 'I've been thinking... why *should* you have to run away? '

'Isaac will kill me if he finds–'

'Not if we can have him arrested first.'

'Arrested? How are we going to–'

'I know a man called Edwards,' Sam said eagerly. 'He's woodsman on the Atterley estate – he lives not far from Coalport in a cottage in the forest. He came to speak to Yates when there was stealing the last time. He's a part-time constable, paid by Wenlock bailiffs to keep the peace. If we were to tell Edwards it's *Isaac* doing the thieving, well, he'll arrest him an' you'll be rid of the devil for good.'

'What if the constable–'

'What are you waiting for? Let's go look for him. He'll catch Isaac an' then the villain will be hanged or sent to the colonies. Either way you'll be rid of him. Then you can go home.'

'What if Edwards doesn't believe us? Isaac will say he's done nothing wrong. Then Edwards will believe *him*, and we'll be the ones in trouble,' I said.

'All we have to do is tell the constable what the men are up to. Then he'll catch 'em. Come on,' he said, jumping to his feet, 'tomorrow's Sunday, so we dunna sail for Worcester till the day after.'

I was about to follow him when I tripped over the ends of the flapping stockings. 'Wait a minute – my clothes,' I cried.

Sam hurried into the kitchen and came back holding out my boots. 'The soles have dried by the stove, but your other stuff is still wet. I'll hide your clothes in the storeroom. They'll be out of sight till they dry. No need to worry, you can keep my things as long as you like,' he said cheerfully, with a wave of his huge hand.

I nodded gratefully. While Sam was gone to the storeroom, I folded the flapping bits of stocking under my feet and shoved my feet into my boots. Then stuffing the bottoms of my borrowed canvas trousers into the tops of my boots, I tied the laces. Taking one last long look around the *Emily,* where Dad had been so happy, I slowly left the cabin.

It was much colder in the hold after the warmth from the stove. Hurrying up the ladder after Sam, I climbed over the gunnel and dropped down onto the quay beside him. It was almost dark, mist was slowly gathering between the riverbanks. The light from the oil lamps along the quay splintered and shivered across the surface of the dark, deep river. Scudding clouds crossed the moon, patterning the quay with moving patches of silver and deep black shadow. The raw, damp air made me shiver. I pulled Sam's jumper closer to me.

There were few people about, work being over for the day. Most of the watermen had gone to their cottages, or were making their way to *The Tumbling Sailor*. Over at Coalbrookdale, the sky above the gorge glowed dull red and orange from the furnaces and burning coal heaps.

On the other side of the quay, through a gap between the warehouses, I saw part of the village street and the front of *The Tumbling Sailor*. From the bottle glass windows of the inn, lamplight shone out on the cobbles. Singing, and wild shouting was spilling out into the sharp night air, and silhouetted in the open doorway of the taproom was Isaac Whitlock.

10

No Way Out!

Choking with fear, I grabbed Sam's arm and dragged him down into the shadows, close under the hull of the *Emily*. My heart beating hard, my skin crawling with fear, I pointed towards the inn.

Isaac was pacing up and down in front of the *Sailor*. Then he crossed the village street, walking swiftly through the gap between the warehouses towards me. I shrank back, my whole body trembling as he reached the end of the warehouse wall. Then turning the corner, he strode off down the quay and didn't look back. He hadn't seen me.

'That's him. That was Isaac,' I whispered, shaking Sam's arm.

'Good. Now's our chance to see what he's up to,' Sam hissed back. 'Let's follow him.'

'Don't be mad – it's too dangerous,' I muttered in alarm. 'I thought we are going to find the constable and tell him about the thieving?'

'If we follow Isaac we can see what he's up to – find where he's hiding the stolen goods. Then we can show the constable an' he'll *have* to believe us,' Sam said. Scrambling to his feet, he hurried off towards the end of the quay before I could stop him.

His boots made an awful noise on the cobbles. I called after him as loudly as I dared, telling him to go quietly, but he kept clumping along and didn't stop. Peering anxiously after him, I thought I saw him turn and wave at me. Then he was gone.

I was worried what might happen to him and scared and angry at his foolishness. Despite my terrible fear of Isaac, I had to follow Sam. He'd saved me from drowning and now he was in danger because of me. I was doing nothing to stop him.

Forcing myself to get to my feet, I walked slowly along the quay, ready to turn and run, when a dark shape sprang at me from behind a row of coal wagons. I struggled violently and heard an urgent voice hiss, 'Keep still, it's me, Sam!'

He let go, a broad grin on his face, and I growled, 'That wasn't funny. I thought you–'

'Shsss!' he said in what he seemed to think was a whisper, 'over there.'

Looking to where he was pointing, I saw the dark outline of

Lloyd, the fat bellied banksman. He was struggling to push a handcart with squeaking wheels towards the large warehouse at the end of the quay, but the wheels stuck on the cobbles. There was a sudden movement, close to the side door of the warehouse, and Isaac came from the shadows and strode swiftly towards him.

Seizing one of the handles, Isaac shoved the cart so violently that it shot forward, dragging the squealing banksman after it. Then snarling at Lloyd to follow him, Isaac marched back to the warehouse and gave a quick look along the quay. I heard the rattle of a chain, the sound of a key turning in a lock, and then a door grating on cobbles. Moments later, the banksman pushed the cart into the building and Isaac followed him, swiftly closing the door after them.

'I'd love to know what they are up to,' Sam said. 'Let's see if we can find a window an' look inside.'

'No. It's too dangerous,' I whispered. 'Isaac is bigger than we are. He's got the banksman to help in a fight. While they're in there we must find the constable's cottage and tell him about the thieving.'

'I could beat that fat bellied pudding with one hand behind my back,' Sam said scornfully, 'but I dunna care to fight a man like Isaac. Though I'd do it if I had to. I say we find out where they're hiding the stuff. Then show Edwards an' he'll have to believe us.'

I tried to argue with Sam, telling him it was too dangerous, that Isaac had a knife, but he took no notice. He settled down behind the coal wagons and refused to budge. I waited impatiently beside him for what seemed a very long time. I was growing more and more annoyed at his recklessness. The icy cobbles were striking cold through my bones. The dark grew deeper, and at last, I muttered, 'We could have found the constable by now. It'll be morning soon, then–'

I stopped in alarm. The side door of the warehouse opened suddenly and made me jump. In the flickering light from the oil lamps and the thin shafts of moonlight, I saw the two men struggling to push the cart through the door onto the quay. Isaac was cursing, the banksman was frantically heaving on the handles. It was laden with packing cases and harder to push than ever.

Lloyd was shoving like a mad thing, thudding his belly against the pile of boxes. One of the tea chests was tight against the edge of the door. I could feel Sam shaking with laughter. I dug him in the ribs, terrified he'd give our hiding place away.

'What's the matter? What do you think you're doing, you fool? Can't you steer straight?' It was Isaac's voice, wild and menacing. You could hear the rage in him. Then with a shout, he gave the banksman a violent shove in the back. The cart shot through the warehouse door and onto the quay with Lloyd clinging to the handles.

Closing the door behind him, Isaac fastened the chain, turned the key in the lock, and marched up to Lloyd, waving his clenched fist under the man's nose. 'Get out of the way, you useless idiot. I'll push this time. Just see if you can keep the boxes from falling off!' he growled.

Knocking Lloyd savagely out of the way, Isaac grabbed the cart's handles, bumping it violently over the cobbles. A large wooden chest, perched on top of some barrels, started to slide. Isaac yelled at the banksman to help him. Lloyd lumbered forward, tried to catch hold of the chest, but it was too heavy for him and it crashed to the ground.

The lid flew off, sending clouds of tea leaves shooting into the air. They rained down on Lloyd, making a dark, softly rippling river at his feet. Isaac gave a terrible growl in his throat. Lowering the legs of the handcart, he thundered, 'Don't just stand there, you fat bellied oaf. Do something!'

Puffing and panting, the banksman struggled to turn the tea chest the right way up. Then with frightened bleating noises, he used his hands to scoop up the tea leaves, but they kept trickling through his fingers. Wild with fury, Isaac gave Lloyd a kick, sending him sprawling. Snatching up the banksman's hat, he used it to sweep up the tea and began furiously tipping it back into the chest.

The banksman clambered to his feet, trying to help, all the time getting in the way. Isaac cursed savagely. The little man stepped back, nervously wringing his pudgy hands. He hopped desperately from one boot to the other until Isaac had hurled the last of the tea leaves into the chest. Then hammering the lid down with his fist, he barked at Lloyd, ordering him to help lift the chest back onto the cart.

Isaac was stronger and taller than Lloyd was. The smaller man was struggling to hold on to his side of the tea chest and staggering about. It looked so funny I felt laughter bubbling up inside me. I could feel Sam shaking so much he'd stuffed his fist into his mouth to stop from laughing out loud. By the time Isaac had heaved the chest back on top of the cart, and they'd set off again with their heavy burden, Sam and me had tears of silent laughter running down our faces.

We saw the two men stop several times, frantically trying to steady the boxes. This made us shake with laughter again. It wasn't until they'd turned into one of the alleyways between the warehouses, and the squeaking sound from the cart's wheels

101

faded into the distance, that Sam spluttered, 'Serves 'em right if the cart squashes 'em. Let's go an' see where they're taking the stuff.'

He was about to scramble to his feet, still giggling and hiccupping, when I grabbed hold of him and held him back. 'No need to,' I said. 'That was the banksman with Isaac – he keeps the keys to the pit bank sheds – so they're probably hiding the stuff there. They'll take the path through the woods beside the old plateway, up the hill to the pit bank. It'll take ages with that heavy cart. We've plenty of time to find the constable and tell him what they're up to.'

'Nah... let's follow them,' Sam said. 'Then we'll take something from one of the wooden boxes, show it to Edwards, an' he'll *have* to believe us.'

'It's too dangerous, he'll think *we're* the thieves – I'm going to find the constable.' I struggled to my feet, suddenly feeling very tired. Ignoring the ache in my cold body, and Sam's pleading for me to come back, I hurried as fast as I could towards the end of the quay.

I hadn't gone far when I heard a terrible clatter that echoed horribly around the valley, followed by the sound of Sam cursing loudly. Looking back in alarm, I saw he must have collided with one of the empty wagons on the plateway. He was clutching his shin and hopping up and down. Thinking Isaac and all of Coalport must have heard him, I looked back towards the dark entrance into the alleyway, expecting Isaac and the banksman to come running onto the quay. But although I was rooted to the spot with fear, no one came.

Sighing with relief, I angrily beckoned Sam to follow me. Then hurrying to the end of the quay, I climbed down the steps onto the muddy path beside the river. I hadn't gone far along the riverbank, and was telling myself that I didn't care if Sam came with me or not, when I heard him tramping along the path behind me. He was slipping in the mud and cussing about the overhanging bushes tearing at his hat.

It wasn't long before the light from the oil lamps on the quay, and the huge black shapes of the warehouses were far behind us. I was secretly relieved Sam was coming with me. His angry muttering was a comforting sound in this lonely place. Closed in by tangled trees that crowded the water's edge, we were entering the ghostly, rustling world of the riverside. Once an owl flew over me. I heard the soft down beat of its wings against the air as it passed close to my head. In the moonlight, we were two giant black shadows marching along the surface of the river.

Trailing branches whipped against our faces. Sam plodded behind me, cursing each time nettles stung him or brambles tore at his skin. I didn't say anything to him. I was still angry with him for not wanting to come with me to find the constable. But hearing him stumbling about I warned him to keep well away from the thick clumps of grass along the edge of the path. They hid a steep drop to the river.

Now and then, the slight plop of fish jumping for flies, and the scuttle and squeal of small creatures hunting on the bank, broke the silence. Stumbling along, I heard Sam muttering about wasting time, saying that we should have followed Isaac. I was furiously muttering back, telling him to shut up, when further down the gorge towards Jackfield, on our side of the river, I saw a faint light flickering through the trees, high up on the bank.

'Look, Sam, do you see it?' I cried. 'Maybe it's the constable's cottage.'

'What good is that? What if it isn't his cottage an' we've come all this way for nothing? I told you we should have–'

'Shssss. Did you hear that?'

'Hear what?'

'Listen – I think we're being followed.'

'Maybe it's a fox,' Sam said, but he'd scarce finished speaking when we heard a yell, a loud splash, and a high-pitched voice squealing for help.

'I think the man with the fat belly has fallen in the river,' Sam said with the chuckle.

Moments later, there was more splashing, followed by the sound of Isaac cursing. The hairs on the back of my neck prickled with fear and I cried, 'Run Sam!'

Desperate to reach the cottage, I fled down the path. Sam's feet thudded close behind me. Torn by brambles growing along the bank I ran until my lungs were burning. Gasping for breath, I was growing more and more frantic. The light from the cottage never seemed to come any closer. Thinking Isaac couldn't be far behind me, I gave up any hope of finding the constable, and calling urgently to Sam to follow me, I left the path and started to climb the bank.

Plunging into the trees, I scrambled up the steep side of the gorge. Charging through bushes, I ducked under low branches. Stung by whipping saplings, I clambered higher and higher, pushing through tangled undergrowth. It was so steep in places I had to grab at boulders to stop myself from toppling backwards. Searching for handholds in the rocks, my fear of Isaac gave me the strength to fight my way up the hill.

Pulling myself over a fallen tree, I found a place where the ground levelled out. It was a flat shelf covered in hawthorn bushes and I waded through them, wondering which direction to take, when the ground suddenly dropped away from under me.

Gasping with fear, I came to rest on smooth pebbles and mud at the bottom of the slope. I'd slithered down a dried riverbed over stones, twigs, and leaves. Moments later, Sam somersaulted past me, thudding on his back with much wild cursing.

We had fallen down a steep bank into a moonlit hollow, full of deep black shadows and the stumps of long felled trees. Sam was scrambling about in foxgloves looking for his hat. I listened fearfully for any sound of the men following us up the hill and realised with growing excitement that I knew where I was.

Jumping up and wiping away the blood trickling down my face from a cut on my forehead, I waded over trailing blackberry stems. Then tugging at grasses and small shrubs on the side of the bank, I called urgently to Sam to help me and trod on something hard. Looking down, I saw the handle of a rusty shovel sticking out from a bunch of nettles. Now certain I was in the right place, I tore violently at the tangle of plants, shouting at Sam to come and search.

Sam waded through the brambles, putting on his hat and muttering that now was *not* the time to be looking for blackberries. What did I think I was doing?

Furious with him for not helping, I pulled frantically at more and more strands of ivy and gave a cry of relief. At the bottom of the bank, half hidden by wiry roots and grasses was a hole just

big enough for a man to crawl into it. Wooden posts, now long rotted, supported the entrance. Urgently telling Sam to follow me, I crawled inside.

Banging my back on the roof timbers, I brought down soil on top of me. There was a rusted plateway digging into my knees. The wood shoring up the roof looked ready to collapse, but desperate to hide from Isaac, I crawled forward as fast as I could, struck my head against something hard, and could go no further.

'Stop pushing,' I whispered angrily to Sam who was scrabbling about behind me. 'There's a wagon blocking the tunnel but I think we're far enough in – the moonlight can't reach us here.'

'We should have kept running,' Sam grumbled, 'there's little air in here – what's this place?'

'It's an old adit mine. I used to play here with Maria when I was little. It's where men dug for coal without the landowner knowing what they–'

We heard a crash. A loud oath rang out, not far from where we were hiding. 'Sounds like Isaac's fallen down the bank –

serves him right,' Sam muttered.

'Shsss. He'll hear you,' I whispered fiercely.

The roof was so low we had to sit with our heads bent and our knees up to our chins. We stayed very still, cramped up close together in the hole as the sound of feet swishing through the long grass came closer.

'I'm wet through and I'm freezing – it'll soon be dawn – we've still got to move the cart.' It was the banksman's whining voice.

'Stop your moaning. You should look where you're going. It's not my fault that you're a clumsy idiot. Keep looking. They're here somewhere. When I find them I'll silence them for good!' Isaac snarled. 'They're close, look, the grass is trodden flat. Are you going to help me look, or not?'

I heard the banksman give a frightened yelp. Then to my horror, I saw Isaac's head and shoulders filling the entrance to tunnel, blocking out most of the moonlight. Trembling with fear, I pressed my back against the wagon, trying to make myself as small as possible. I felt Sam shuffling closer. I was shaking violently, thinking Isaac would crawl in after me and drag me out. Then I saw shafts of moonlight spilling into the mouth of the adit again and he was gone.

I waited, scared what he might do next. Moments later, I

heard the clang of a shovel. There was the sound of splintering wood and the rattle of earth and stones. The light at the entrance of the tunnel went out like a snuffed candle. Sam and me were trapped in the dark.

11

Wild with Anger

For one terrible moment, I thought I was back in Blists Hill mine after the explosion with bits of coal hitting me. But it was Sam. He was showering me with soil and small pebbles and I had to stop him.

'Don't,' I shouted, 'what are you up to? You'll bring the roof down on top of us – keep still!'

He took no notice of me. 'I'm digging us out of here,' he cried. Frantic to escape, he was too scared to listen. I felt for the back of his jacket, pulling and yelling at him to stop. 'If you keep digging, more of the roof will cave in and smother us – Isaac has knocked down the posts at the entrance – he's brought down the bank!'

'There's no air!' Sam cried. I could hear him scrabbling in the earth, making soil patter around me.

'The more you dig the more air you'll use up,' I said, 'you'll suffocate us. Listen to me. I'll find a way out of here, but not if you bring the roof down.'

Thankfully, his digging stopped. My mind raced, trying to think what to do. Feeling the wagon, hard against my back, gave me an idea. 'Sam. If we move the wagon back onto the plateway, we can ram it through the soil blocking the entrance. Help me lift it.'

There was little room in the tunnel and it was dangerous with Sam squeezed up beside me. We couldn't see what we were doing. We kept knocking against the boards holding up the roof. The wagon was wedged tight against the wall, tilted on its side. As we tugged, we felt a steady stream of soil falling onto us.

'It's hopeless,' Sam said angrily, 'it won't budge and we're bringing down the roof – we'll never move it.'

'It's *not* hopeless. I can feel a gap between the wheels of the wagon and the wall – I think it's wide enough to crawl through to the other side.'

'Dunna be daft,' Sam said miserably. 'What's the good of that? We want to get out, not go deeper.'

'I'm not daft. The men who dug the tunnels made *another* tunnel above the one they were working in – just in case of a roof fall. If we can find it, we'll soon be out of here.'

I didn't tell Sam that I was worried Isaac might have found the escape tunnel and blocked that too. Sam wasn't used to being underground like me. He was terrified enough.

'How big is the gap? I'll never get through,' Sam said miserably.

'It's a bit tight, but I can do it. Then once I'm free I'll dig you out.'

He was muttering something, but I was already trying to squeeze into the narrow space between the wall timbers and the wheels of the wagon, pushing hard with my boots against the plateway. My heart thumped inside me, fearful I'd be stuck and never be able to free myself again, but I kept going.

Twisting my body, I wriggled and wriggled, moving forward hardly at all. I was horribly close to the side of the wagon and so squashed it was difficult to breathe. Pushing with my boots and clinging to the wheels, I realised with sudden horror that I couldn't go forward and I couldn't go back.

'Sam, I can't move,' I said, my voice choking with fear.

I felt him grab my feet. He gave such a hard tug I thought he'd pull my boots off and leave me where I was. His grip on my ankles made them burn with pain. I shouted out but he just gave another fierce pull, I shot backwards, and I was free. The hurt was terrible, but I could breathe again.

'You were supposed to p*ush*, not *pull,*' I muttered angrily, lying there in a crumpled heap and trying to cope with the fierce stabbing pain in my ribs. 'You pulled so hard I'm sure my ribs are broken.'

'How was I to know what you wanted me to do? I thought you wanted me to help you?'

It was no use arguing, and trying to shut out the fear of being trapped again, I started to push and wriggle forward into the gap. This time, when I called to him, he shoved so hard against the soles of my boots I thought my legs would break. There was a searing pain all over my body, then I felt Sam give another push and I was lying on the other side of the wagon.

'Sam, I'm through,' I shouted back to him as I struggled onto my knees, rubbing the tops of my painfully throbbing shoulders. 'You'll soon be out of here, so don't worry. I'll be back and dig you out as fast as I can.'

I started to crawl along the damp passageway and felt a small animal with scratchy feet run over my hand. Trying not to imagine what it was, I hadn't gone much further when something soft and damp brushed against my face. Recoiling in horror, my whole body trembling, I fought my fear, stretched out my hand, and touched what felt like coarse wet hair.

Terrified, but knowing I had to keep going, I pushed my hand into it. It was like the mouth of some slimy animal. Feeling sick in my belly, something spattered all over me. I tried to shield myself, covering my head with my arms, and realised it was soil raining down on me and there was a dull light coming through a hole above my head. I'd found the shaft to the escape tunnel!

The damp hairs dangling around me were just the roots of plants, growing down from the top of the bank. Scared I'd bring down more soil, I saw rotted timber lining the shaft. Just touching it was dangerous.

Scared I'd drown in earth if I stayed there much longer, I struggled to kneel. Then taking a deep breath, I covered my head with my arms and fiercely thrust my body upwards. Soil fell in a terrifying manner, I was waist deep in it, but I fought against its growing weight and felt what was left of a metal ladder. Most of the rungs were gone, but clinging to it, I heaved myself up until I could stand and found I was looking into the upper tunnel.

There wasn't much light, but I could just make out floorboards level with my head. Using the metal ladder, I pulled myself into the escape tunnel, slid onto my belly, and saw moonlight ahead of me. Giving a sigh of relief, for Isaac hadn't blocked the exit after all, I crawled forward slowly, worrying about the pit props on either side of me and wondering if they would collapse.

Fearful I would send more soil tumbling on top of me,

thoughts of Sam alone in the dark below helped me to forget my own worries and to keep going. Moving bit by bit towards the faint beams of moonlight, I reached the end of the tunnel, stretched out my arms, and tore at the roots and brambles that had grown over the exit. Once the gap was big enough, I thrust my head and shoulders through, leaned out as far as I dared, and saw the moon-filled hollow below me.

The escape tunnel was above the entrance to the adit, and sliding head first down the bank, I landed on a heap of soil and rocks, every bone in my body aching, and struggled painfully to my feet. The trees crowding the rim of the hollow were full of silent eerie shadows, I looked nervously around, and stood there listening to the sounds in the forest, but Isaac and the banksman seemed to have gone.

I was fearful Isaac might have carried away the shovel, but I found it in the grass where he'd dropped it. Snatching it up, I stared horrified at the mound of earth, roots, and broken pit props blocking the mouth of the adit, then started to dig as fast as I could. Shovelling soil until the already hurting muscles in my arms, back, and legs were burning more, and sweat was pouring off me, horrible thoughts of Sam choking from bad air, and dying in the dark alone, wouldn't go away.

I don't know how long I was digging, I just kept thrusting my shovel into the heap of soil while the mound never seemed to get any smaller, and I was rubbing sweat out of my eyes, when I realised that the mound *was* smaller. Some of the heap had started to slide and part of the bank above the entrance to the adit had appeared. Eagerly, I shouted Sam's name but heard nothing.

I was desperately shouting, when I saw a small hole appear in the mound in front of me. Soil began to trickle from it, the hole grew steadily bigger, and the top of Sam's hat came through. Then to my delight and great relief, I saw his muddy face.

Soft earth erupted around him, and he crawled out, looking like a large mole wearing a jacket and waistcoat. Climbing stiffly to his feet, soil poured off him like water from the pump. In the moonlight, he looked pale under his freckles, but he staggered towards me, a delighted grin on his broad face, and thumped me on the back.

'Ouch!' I cried, 'that hurts!'

We were grinning at each other, jumping about like mad things and we couldn't stop laughing. It took us a long time before we calmed down a bit. Then, very solemnly, we shook hands.

'Thanks' he said, 'I thought it were the end of me.' Then he went suddenly quiet, and in a strange, hard voice that didn't sound like Sam at all he said, 'Isaac near killed us in that tunnel.

I dunna care how long it takes, I'll catch that evil creature an' have him put behind bars, you'll see!'

I'd never seen Sam angry before, and he looked so fierce. Then he straightened his muddy hat. Pressing it firmly onto his head, he climbed rapidly up the side of the bank and out of the hollow. Beckoning me to follow, he disappeared into the trees and I heard him charging down the hill. He was crashing through the forest, leaving a trail of twigs and broken branches. When I finally caught up with him on the riverbank, he was looking towards the faint light shining through the trees.

'Let's find that cottage,' he said. Not waiting for me to answer, he strode off down the path. I tried to keep up with him, but it was like following farmer Althorpe's prize bull. The day the animal had been stung on the nose by bees and had broken loose, trampling the pigsty.

He was some way ahead of me when I saw him leave the path. When I managed to catch sight of him, he was climbing up the bank into the trees. He was pounding up the hill at a frantic rate. I followed him as fast as I could. Then the trees thinned a little and ahead of me was the dark outline of a stone cottage with smoke drifting from the chimney.

Finding a track that led to a gate in a low fence, I followed Sam along a pebbled path. He was muttering at me to hurry up.

There was no light from the window at the front of the cottage. Turning a corner of the building into the back yard, we heard a dog barking fiercely. It made us both jump.

The animal was flinging himself about in a shed next to the privy, desperate to get at us. I hoped very hard it wouldn't escape. There was lamplight shining through the grimy kitchen window, and Sam strode forward, raised his huge fist, and thumped hard on the door.

12

Blood, Birds, and Butterflies

The dog was barking fit to burst. We waited and waited. No one came. We were about to leave when we heard shuffling footsteps inside the cottage. Then a woman's voice shouted to quieten the animal, and in the sudden hush that followed she called out, 'Go away, he's not here.'

'Isaac Whitlock is robbing the warehouse. So Edwards had better come quick an' catch the robbers,' Sam shouted.

There was the sound of a key turning in the lock, bolts sliding back, and a woman's head popped out through the door opening like a jack-in-the-box I'd seen at the fair. Her white hair tied in curling rags made her look ghostly in the moonlight. We stepped back a bit because she gave us both a fright.

'He's not here,' she muttered. 'Went to the mine about the explosion – he's not back yet – be off with you.' Then her head popped back in again. The door slammed shut, and we heard the key grating in the lock.

I looked at Sam who seemed as astonished as I did. Then without a word, we walked back down the path, through the gate and onto the hill. We hadn't gone far when we started to splutter with nervous laughter.

'Thought it were a ghost,' Sam said. He darted his head about and kept saying in silly voice, 'He's not here, be off with you,' and we laughed till our sides ached and felt better.

'What are we going to do now?' I said. We'd reached the bottom of the hill and were staring at the dark swirling river. 'I can't go back to Coalport. Isaac will be looking for me at first light, and–'

'You're coming back to Coalport with me,' Sam said fiercely. 'He's not going to drive you away if I can help it. He nearly killed me too, an' if you hadn't known about an adit, or whatever you call it, we'd have been left there to die. We'll go back to Coalport, look for the constable, an' he'll catch Isaac up to his thieving.'

'It must soon be dawn. If Isaac has got any sense, he'll have gone home by now. He won't still be thieving.'

'Maybe, maybe not,' Sam said. 'He'll keep thieving as long as he can, I figure. If not, we're sure to meet the constable on his way home an' we'll tell him about the robbery – come on.'

120

Tired, and still worrying whether the constable would believe us, I trudged after Sam along the path. I was thinking it would be best to take off across the fields. No one would believe our story the way we looked, covered with mud.

At every step, my tiredness grew. My body ached so much I longed to curl up somewhere in the trees. I wanted to go to sleep and forget all the misery in my head. I hardly noticed the walk back to the village. Putting one tired foot in front of the other, I was startled and surprised to see a warehouse loom up in front of me and realised we were back at Coalport already.

Listening to the slap of the river against the sides of the vessels and the creak of the hawsers, I watched Sam climbing the steps onto the quay. Reluctantly following him, and longing for sleep, I heard something that brought me suddenly very much awake. Hurrying after him, I grabbed his arm, whispering fiercely, 'It's Isaac. Can't you hear the cart wheels squeaking?'

'They're still up to their stealing, told you so,' Sam said gleefully, turning his head to grin at me in the moonlight. Shaking me off, he tiptoed loudly across the cobbles. Beckoning me to follow him, he disappeared down an alleyway between the warehouses.

Alarmed at the noise he was making, I was scared Isaac would see him. I followed at a distance, keeping to the shadows against a warehouse wall. Moments later, Sam hurried back to me, saying in a loud whisper, 'It's all right. They're a long way off. If we hurry, we can catch them up. We'll see where they are taking the stuff, find the constable, an' tell him. Then you'll be free of Isaac – you can go home. That's what you want, isn't it?'

I was too exhausted, miserable, and too worried about my dad to argue with him. I just trailed after him into the shadow-filled alleyway, along the fronts of the cottages, and crossed the bridge onto the moonlit road to Ironbridge. Following behind him, I kept close to the hedge, listening to the sounds of the river, Sam's noisy boots, and the faint creaking of the cart. In the distance were two humped-back shadowy figures struggling with their burden. We were just in time to see them turn from the road and take the path into the woods.

'They're following the old plateway to the pit bank,' I muttered to Sam, but he was already hurrying down the road and disappearing into the trees after the men. I followed him into the forest. Climbing wearily up the bank, I longed to be in my bed, pulling the old blanket over my head, but it was no use wishing.

I found him crouched in undergrowth beside an oak tree. I could see the top of his hat sticking up out of the bushes. He was dangerously close to the path where the banksman and Isaac were struggling with the cart on the hill, moving in and out of patches of moonlight. I whispered at Sam to be careful, but he was already off again, moving clumsily through the undergrowth.

Once the men stopped for a rest, and I realised I was not far from the row of cottages where I lived. Through the trees, I could just see the roof and the top of my bedroom window. I was hoping my sisters were safe asleep and Dad was safe home with Mum in the back bedroom. I was longing to find out, but the men were on the move again. Reluctantly following them, I caught up with Sam as Isaac and the banksman reached the top of the hill.

The men were climbing the pit bank towards the sheds and workshops, struggling with the heavily laden cart. The wheels were sinking into the loose coal and stones. They were cursing and it took them a long time to move the cart again. But finding a bit of firmer ground they pushed it through a gap between the workshops towards the canal.

Crouched close to the pithead, Sam was about to follow them. I whispered I knew a better way. Leading him along a track between the side of the tommy shop and the chain maker's hut, I brought him out at the back of the workshops, onto a path further down the canal.

Crouching beside the chain maker's workshop, we saw the coal shed next to the engine house had its door swinging open.

123

Isaac and the banksman were unloading the boxes and barrels from the cart. They were struggling to roll the larger barrels through the open doorway and Isaac was cursing and snarling at Lloyd to help him.

It took them a long time before they'd moved all the goods into the shed. But at last, the cart was empty and we heard its wheels squeaking as the men left the pit bank and pushed it back down the hill towards the Coalport Road.

'They're off to fetch another load,' Sam said. 'Now we'll take some of what they stole and show the policeman.'

'No, they might come back,' I warned him, 'besides, it can't be long till morning and–'

He shook his head. 'Nah! They'll be going for more. They won't give up till they really have to. It'll take them ages to load up again. You saw how long it took them to push the cart up the hill.'

Jumping up, he ran along the canal path to the coal shed and waved at me excitedly. I trudged after him and heard him shout, 'Look Josh, they've left the padlock on the door and they've left the key in it!'

It didn't take him long to turn the key, unhook the chain, and disappear into the shed. I was scared the men might come back. Hearing him muttering something, I anxiously followed him inside. He was climbing over heaps of coal that covered most of the floor. He was slipping and sending up clouds of thick black dust. Reaching the top of the heap, he dug in the coal with his huge hands, sending large pieces bumping and rolling down towards me and I had to jump out of the way.

'The stuff's here somewhere,' he cried angrily, throwing more and more coal around. Then he gave a shout. Bending down, he tugged at a piece of canvas like a dog shaking a rat and cried, 'I've found it. Josh, take a look at this.'

'Come down. Isaac will be back and catch us!'

'I'm not stopping now,' Sam cried, 'we've a chance to show the constable what they've stole.' Pulling at something under the canvas, his feet slipping on the loose pieces of coal, he tugged at the end of what looked like a long bundle of sailcloth. Then giving a mighty heave, he dragged it free and sent it rolling down the heap towards me.

'They were hiding the stuff under the coal,' he cried triumphantly, sliding dangerously to the floor with coal bouncing everywhere. Bending down, he struggled with the rope round the sailcloth covering the bundle, making impatient noises, for the knots were tight. He looked around, noticed broken glass in the small window frame, and made a grab for it. Letting out a yell, he sucked him hand.

'It's your own fault you've cut yourself,' I said angrily. 'You should have waited and told the constable. Here, let's see what you've done.'

He took no notice of me. In the bit of moonlight coming through the window he'd seen something on the floor. Snatching it up he cried, 'This'll do.'

It was a bit of broken knife blade, so blunt that it took him a long time to saw through the knotted ropes with it, but finally the

 strands parted. Eagerly pulling back the rough canvas, he found a further covering of soft white linen inside.

'Let's see what's in that,' he said, and gave a gasp of surprise. There was another roll of cloth, but it was like nothing I'd ever seen before. Sam found the end of it and lifted it up. It was so thin you could see through it. It was like the embroidered tablecloth the Lady at the big house gave Mum when she left to be married. But it was much thinner. There were tiny birds and butterflies all over it, the wings stitched with something that shone in the moonlight.

'It's lovely – we really shouldn't be doing this,' I said.

'There's something on the outside,' Sam said, lifting the edge of the sailcloth wrapping, 'can you read?'

126

I nodded, turning the sacking over so that the moonlight shone onto it, and slowly read the words, '*Sir Ed-mund Att-er-ley, Att-er-ley Hall.*'

Sam nodded. 'I've heard of him.' He was sucking his hand. Spots of blood were dripping onto the birds and butterflies. Before I could stop him, he ripped off a piece from the beautiful cloth and tied it tight round his hand.

'You shouldn't have–'

I didn't have a chance to say any more. I think we heard the sound of the squeaking cart at the same time. It was coming along the path towards the shed. We looked at each other in alarm. It was too late to run. Seeing nowhere to hide, I hastily shut the door. Crouched on the floor beside Sam, I expected the door to open, Isaac to grab me, and haul me out.

13

Betrayal

'You fool. You didn't drop the key on the bank – you left it in the lock!' Isaac bellowed.

I heard the banksman give a yelp, the chain rattled on the door, and the key turned in the lock. Then there was the sound of the squeaking cart as the men walked away.

'That's done it,' Sam said, as we struggled to our feet. 'They've locked the door. How are we going to get out of here? Do you think you could climb through that small window?'

'It's your fault,' I snapped at him, 'you *would* go into the shed. I told you–'

I stopped, for Sam was making a weird choking sound and pointing to the window. I turned and saw a ghostly face staring at me through the broken glass. It looked so awful with the moon full on it that I took a step back, gasping with fright.

Then the face was gone. Moments later I heard a dull thud and clutched Sam's arm, my heart hammering with fear. The coal shed door opened and I shrank back, but it was only my sister Maria. She stood in the doorway, laughing at me and holding a large stone in one fist and the broken lock in the other.

Angry with her for the fright she'd given me, I marched out of the shed after Sam without saying a word. Ignoring us both, she was off down the pit bank into the woods. We followed her through the trees until she stopped by an old beech, one that had its branches close to the ground, and she scuttled under it. Sam and me crawled after her and settled down in the prickling twigs and heaps of rustling leaves.

'You looked terrified,' she said with a giggle and giving me a push. 'You looked really scared.' Then she peered at Sam, trying to see him in the little moonlight reaching the forest floor. 'Who's he?'

'It's Sam, he's a friend.'

'What's he done to his hand?'

'What are you doing here, Maria? Have you heard any news – is Dad safe?' I asked quickly.

'They're still trapped.'

The shock of her words hit me hard. I'd tried to tell myself I was worrying for nothing. That the men were free and Dad was safe at home already, but now all hope left me. Recovering a little from my misery, I said, 'What are you doing here?'

'Huh,' she said angrily. 'Good thing I did come along, you have a coal sieve for a memory, Josh. I *told* you I'd creep out at night and keep a look out for you. I managed to leave without waking Sara. When you didn't come back, I decided to go down to Coalport and look for you. I was on my way down the old plateway when I saw Isaac and Lloyd pushing the cart up the hill. I hid in the trees. I saw the tea chests and knew they were thieving. Then I saw you and *him*,' she nodded at Sam, 'coming up the bank after them.'

'Is Mum all right, and Sara?'

'Mum's found out about Isaac's stealing. What he's really like, but he threatens her – says she'll be sent to the colonies for taking the soap and twists of tea he gave her. He's going to move into the cottage with us and send Sara to work on the pit bank if Mum tells on him, so she–'

I grabbed her arm. There was a light flickering through the trees, coming up the hill. The beam was swinging about, close to the ground. Someone was carrying a lantern. 'Quick, Maria, it might be Isaac. You don't want him to see you. Be off home as fast as you can,' I whispered.

She gave me a quick hug, crawled from under the tree, and silently disappeared. Sam was already hurrying through the trees

130

towards the moving lantern. I followed him, grabbing his jacket. 'Be careful. Let's see who it is first,' I warned him.

Coming close to the edge of the clearing, we crouched in the

undergrowth and saw a woodsman in leather jerkin and breeches, his face hidden by the brim of his woollen hat. He was walking steadily up the path, a stout staff in one hand, and the lantern in the other.

'That's Edwards,' Sam said, springing to his feet. Hurrying from the bushes, he ran onto the bank, but he hadn't gone far when he came to a sudden halt. I was so close behind him I nearly bumped into the back of him and heard his sharp intake of breath. The constable was not alone. Striding up the hill behind him was Isaac, and puffing and panting a short distance behind him was Lloyd the banksman.

Isaac saw me, shook his fist, and shouted, 'Constable, that's the pair thieving from the warehouse!'

Sam and I turned to run, but in our panic, we ran into each other. Isaac strode forward and grabbed me by the arm, wrenching it painfully. Sam seized hold of my other arm and held on tight. Isaac tried to drag me one way, but Sam pulled me in another. They started a tug of war. They jerked me violently from side to side and just when I thought they would pull me in half, I saw Edwards stride up to Sam, his staff raised to strike.

'Sam!' I cried.

Sam moved swiftly and the staff flew past his head, hitting the ground. Now the banksman lumbered towards him, trying to seize hold of him, but Sam hurled himself at the fat man and they rolled down the bank into the trees.

Isaac shoved me towards Edwards shouting, 'You're supposed to be the law round here, arrest him for breaking into the warehouse.'

'It's a lie. Isaac is stealing, not us. You look in the coal shed – you'll see what he's taken,' I cried.

Sam staggered out of the trees, angrily punching dents out of his hat and ramming it back on his head. Edwards peered at Sam, holding up his lantern to see him better. 'I know you. You're on the *Emily Grey*,' he said. 'I'll be having a word with your maister. He doesn't know what a thieving wretch he employs.'

'You'd best look in the coal shed first,' Sam said threateningly. 'Josh is telling the truth, *we're* not thieving.' He pointed to Isaac who was digging his nails into the back of my neck. 'Him with the beard an' that other fat bellied one – the one

132

I gave a hiding to in the trees just now. They are the ones taking stuff from the warehouse. We followed them up the hill. Saw them hiding what they'd stolen in the coal shed. You ask your wife. We went to your cottage to tell her.'

'I'm the constable, so dunna you be telling me what to do,' Edwards said, raising his staff. 'You've no right going bothering my wife.' Then to my horror, I saw him wink at Isaac Whitlock and Whitlock wink back.

'What's your name?' Edwards asked Sam. 'Well, whoever you are, you're coming with me to the bailiff at Wenlock – that's the both of you,' he added turning to me. He was pulling me away from Isaac when Sam punched the constable hard on the jaw, making Edwards loose his hold on my arm as he fell.

'Sam!' I yelled as Isaac charged towards him.

Sam turned and fled into the forest. I followed him, running headlong, leaping over bushes, and frantically weaving in and out of the trees. Scratched and hit by low branches, I ducked as best I could, all the time trying to keep up with Sam and hearing Isaac shouting somewhere in the forest behind me.

Gasping for breath, I forced myself to run on despite the pain in my chest. Sam was crashing through the undergrowth ahead of me. I don't know how deep we were in the forest, or how long we had been running, but I could hardly breathe. I couldn't go much further, I had to slow down a little and it was then I realised Isaac's shouting had stopped.

Still scared he was close by, I listened hard, but there was no sound of anyone coming along the forest track. The only thing I heard was a painful wheezing in my chest and the pattering of small creatures in the undergrowth. From time to time I jumped nervously, and wondering what had happened to Sam I saw the first dawn light filtering through the tree canopy.

Thinking the men must have given up searching for us, I risked calling softly for Sam, and it wasn't long before I saw him walking down the track towards me. Without a word, we found a space in a clump of elder bushes and sat down for a rest. With the chorus of birdsong around us, we were busy with our own thoughts for a while. Then I said, 'Sam, I've made up my mind. I shall go to Wenlock and try to find work.'

'You'd better clean yourself up first, if you want someone to take you on,' Sam said with a grin. 'You should see yourself, you're covered with soil and coal dust from the shed.'

'What about you – you're in a mess, too,' I said indignantly. We peered at each other and hooted with laughter.

'Dunna know what I'll do,' Sam said with a heavy sigh when we'd stopped laughing and were serious again. 'If I go back to Coalport, the constable knows who I am. He's friendly with the maister. If the maister believes I've been stealing, he'll have me shipped out to the colonies or worse. I'd best come with you, look for work on a farm, or on the canals...'

'I'm sorry, Sam – if you hadn't saved me from the river none of this would have happened to you.'

'Dunna fret yourself,' he said cheerfully. 'If it's to be Wenlock, you'd best lead the way. I dunna know these woods.'

'There's a track that'll bring us out to the Brockton road. If I can find it. It's not far from there to the Wood Bridge at Coalport. There'll be few about on the road at this hour, being Sunday. We can cross the bridge and be on the coach road to Wenlock without being seen.'

Sam nodded, and after climbing wearily to my feet, I led Sam along several forest trails that took us nowhere. Feeling disheartened and thinking we'd be wandering in the forest all day, I eventually came across a small clearing. It was criss-crossed by several tracks and there was one that looked more used than the others. Following this, and feeling more hopeful, I tried not to listen to Sam's complaining that I was leading him in circles and realised we were close to the edge of the wood.

In a short while, we left the trees behind and could see open farmland. In the distance was the church at Brockton, and following a path along the edge of a wheat field, we climbed over a stile onto the Brockton road, both of us too tired to say anything.

Reaching the Wood Bridge at Coalport before the sun was fully up we plodded over it, listening to our boots echoing hollowly on the roadway planks. The sun glinted on the Severn beneath us as we crossed over, and I looked down at Coalport quay. I saw a lad driving cattle through the water meadows nearby, but there were few people about.

At the other side of the bridge, we began the long walk to Wenlock and I felt better with Coalport village left behind me. Sam kept looking back towards the river and I guessed he must be thinking about the *Emily Grey* as much as I was thinking and worrying about Dad. I wondered if Sam was bothered about the constable speaking to Yates, or if he was just coming with me out of kindness. It made me feel awful, not knowing whether he was leaving the *Emily* just because of me.

We reached the crest of a hill and here the road descended rapidly, winding between hedges and fields of ripening corn. The sun was high above us, making us hot and sweaty. Finding a stream running alongside the hedge, we stopped for a drink, dipping our hands in the icy water and gulping it down. Then we splashed our faces and heads until most of the coal dust and soil from the adit mine was gone, and we felt less itchy. Sam dipped his hat into the stream, rung the water out of it, and stuck it firmly back on his head.

The sun was high in the sky when we set off again, but soon a fierce wind sprang up, sending heavy rain clouds scurrying across the farmland towards us. It was not long before the first large splashes of rain blew into us, bursting on the dusty road and gurgling along the ditches. Looking towards the distant line of hills, we saw flashes of forked lightening and heard a rumble of thunder.

'There's a cottage over there, in the next field,' I shouted above the sound of the howling wind. 'It looks deserted – we might be able to shelter there until the storm passes.'

Despite how tired we felt, we started to run, splashing through the rainwater running in a steady stream down the middle of the road. The cottage was on the far side of a ploughed field, and climbing over a gate we squelched across the furrows. Our boots caked with mud, it was an effort to lift our feet from the clay. Keeping close to the hedge, we tried to shelter from the worst of the rain blowing into us, but we were wet through by the time we reached a gate in a broken fence.

Knocking as much mud as we could from our boots on a stony path, we hurried past a vegetable plot, overgrown with dock leaves and thistles. Through the driving rain, I saw the thatched roof of the cottage, grey with age and sagging in the middle, but at least it would give us some shelter. The door was hanging almost off its hinges, but Sam lifted it and we squeezed through the gap.

Tripping over each other in our haste to get inside, we heard the mad patter of rats and mice as they darted in all directions across the brick floor. Some dashed into holes in the wainscot, others ran in panic along the beams into the thatch, but we were too wet and tired to care about sharing with such companions. We were just glad to be out of the storm.

It looked as though no one had lived there for many years. The one-roomed cottage was empty, except for a broken stool and a heap of straw in a corner. Sam picked up an old besom, poking the straw, then satisfied there were no rats hiding there, he sat down and I threw myself down beside him.

'We'll have a rest and then go to Wenlock market,' Sam said. He yawned widely as we watched the rain furiously beating against the broken glass in the window opening and trickling down the walls.

Taking off his wet jacket and banging the rain out of his hat, Sam stretched out and made himself comfortable. Rain had soaked through the jumper Sam had given me and I pulled it off, settled in the straw, and dragged some over me for warmth.

I found it hard to sleep. So many thoughts were running through my head. Worrying, I said, 'Sam, do you want to go back to the *Emily*? Do you really want to go on to Wenlock?'

The only answer was a loud snore. He was fast asleep. I envied him. I thought about Dad, Mum, and my sisters, and fearful of what the next days would bring, I fell asleep at last.

14

Thunder

I woke with a start, thinking I was safe in my bedroom at home and looked round for my sisters. Then remembering where I was and feeling miserable, I scrambled to my feet. Shaking off the straw sticking to me, I hurried over to the door.

Peering through the gap, I saw the rain had stopped. A watery sun was breaking through high clouds and I was alarmed to see it must be well past noon. Looking towards a distant rise of land, I noticed a line of elms leading to a big house. It had a steep, stone tiled roof, and there was smoke rising from the tall chimneys. In the next field full of sheep, two men were hedging, but they were so far away I thought we were safe enough.

'I don't know how long we've been asleep,' I said to Sam, who must have heard me moving about and was yawning and sitting up. 'The sun is close to the hills on the other side of the valley. At least it's stopped raining.'

'What's that growing by the hedge beside the road, do you think it's something to eat?' Sam said, coming over to the door and squinting into the sun.

'I think they are carrots. We could pull some up and wash them. There's bound to be a stream running alongside the hedge. But if we're caught–'

'Not bothered about washing,' Sam growled. 'I'm so hungry I'll eat 'em, mud an' all. An' there's no one about to see. Come on.'

He put on his jacket. I pulled on his old jumper. Both of us shivered. The clothes were cold and wet against our skin. Squeezing through the gap in the cottage door, we struggled across the muddy field towards the carrots. It was hard work. There had been so much rain and our boots kept sinking in the sticky mud. Sam was the first to reach the carrots and began pulling them up in handfuls. I bent down to do the same when I heard a man's angry bellow and nearly jumped out of my skin.

Looking round, I couldn't see any one at first. Then through a gap in the hedge, I saw a man in a black riding coat and breeches astride a magnificent black horse with a riding crop in his clenched fist. The man yelled at us again and Sam dropped his carrots and started to run. I tried to run after him, but you can't run fast across a muddy field. Glancing back over my shoulder, I saw the hunter effortlessly clear the gate and gallop towards us, clods of earth flying from its hooves.

Both of us floundered in the clay. It was useless trying to get away. Our boots were stuck fast. We stood back to back as the hunter pounded towards us. It was almost on top of us, its powerful black chest towered above us. I raised my arms to protect myself from the rider's crop, but to my surprise, the blow didn't come.

Pulling the stallion up, the man fought to control the animal as it circled around us, the hooves horribly close. Looking down at Sam the horseman barked, 'Don't I know you?'

'Yes – yes, Sir,' Sam said, ducking to avoid the animal's large head. 'I'm 'prenticed to Mr. Yates, the maister of the *Emily*.'

'I thought I'd seen you on the *Emily*. What are you doing here, stealing my carrots and in such a mess? Who is the muddy wretch with you?'

'My friend Joshua, Sir. His father's trapped in the mine at Blists Hill – Joshua's running away from Isaac Whitlock. Isaac has a knife, he's trying to kill him,' Sam blurted out.

'Whitlock?' the rider said sharply, tapping the riding crop against the hunter's shiny rump. He shifted in the saddle as the stallion moved fretfully under him.

'He's pit bottom steward at the Blists Hill mine, Sir,' I said,

142

blinking in the sunlight glinting off the brass buttons on the rider's coat. I looked up at his face, half hidden by a mass of wiry white hair. 'Whitlock's stealing from the *Emily* – hiding the goods in the shed on the pit bank. I heard him talking to the innkeeper at Coalport. They're going to sell the goods at Wenlock. We told Edwards the constable, but he's friends with Isaac and will take us to the bailiffs in Wenlock if he catches us.'

I looked round at Sam, hoping he'd say something more. Noticing his bandaged hand I cried, 'Sam cut his hand – he's bound it up with some of the stolen cloth we found in the coal shed.'

The rider bent low from the saddle, seized Sam's wrist, and stared hard at the piece of cloth. Although it was covered in soil and stained with blood, you could still see the embroidered butterflies and birds.

'That looks like something that belongs to my wife,' he said grimly, letting go of Sam. 'You'd better return to the *Emily* before she sails, boy. If you have trouble from the master, I'll deal with him. I'm the owner of the trow, and you've no need to fear Whitlock either. I'll put an end to his stealing. You'll not be bothered with *him* again!'

'Sir. Don't trust Edwards,' I said.

'I know how to deal with my own woodsman,' he said sharply. Then with a nod to Sam, he tapped the hunter with the

 heel of his boot, grasping the reigns more firmly, but the animal braced its feet in the mud and lowered its head towards me. Its huge liquid eyes peered into mine, its warm moist breath on my face. It nuzzled me, butted me in the chest, and I sat down hard in the wet clay.

'You know horses, boy?' the man said, bringing the stallion in a tight circle around me. The shiny-skinned beast seized me by the shoulder, lifted me to my feet, and gently nibbled me.

'Never seen Thunder take to a stranger like that before – usually has a shocking temper,' he said, sounding puzzled. He stared at me from under thick bushy white eyebrows as if he meant to see right through me.

'I'm used to horses, Sir,' I muttered, as the stallion sniffed my face. Its whiskers prickled my skin, and I forgot my fear of the rider and reached up to stroke the horse on the nose. 'Not as fine as your hunter, he was only a Welsh cob I led in the pit. He was small but he had a fierce temper. Though it wasn't his fault and I learned how to handle him.'

I looked up at the stallion and thought of poor Drummer pulling the heavy wagons of coal in the dark, his back rubbed raw. I felt sad and upset, for I'd not thought of him for a long time.

'Well, you have a way with horses, I must say.' He hesitated for a moment, then struggling to turn the huge beast, urged it into a gallop. It needed no encouragement. It flew at the hedge, clearing it effortlessly, and I heard its hooves pounding the road and was sad to see it go.

Sam slapped me on the back, grinning at me happily. 'Good thing you know about horses,' he said. 'You're in luck. If he does as he says an' has Isaac arrested you'll soon be able to go home, an' I can go back to the *Emily*.'

'We'd better hurry, or the *Emily* will sail without you,' I said, but he shook his head.

'*Emily* wunna be sailing for a bit. They'll be still loading the pig iron, if this rain hasn't bogged the cart down on the roads. Me, I'm not going anywhere until I've had something to eat.'

We tore up more carrots, and carrying them to the hedge, I washed off the grit and mud in water rushing along the ditch. Sam protested and said he didn't need to, but he did the same as me. With a lap full of carrots, we sat on the bank, eating until our bellies were nicely full and our clothes steamed and dried on our backs. Then struggling across the field, we climbed the gate. Stamping as much mud as we could from our boots, we walked along the road, just as the evening colours of the wild flowers in the hedgerows were growing deeper, and the sun was setting.

By the time we were close to Coalport, the lamps along the quay had been lit, their pale glow making moving splinters of light on the dark surface of the swift flowing river. There were not many people about. The warehouse doors onto the slipway were closed for the night. Loud singing was coming from the open door of *The Tumbling Sailor*, and I saw the dear *Emily,* rising and falling gently at her moorings.

'Looks like they haven't loaded her yet. I'll see if the maister is aboard – if he threatens to turn me off I'll tell him I met Sir Edmund Atterley, he daren't go against the owner's wishes,' Sam said with a chuckle. 'You come with me. I'll ask him about you sailing with us one day.'

He set off along the quay. I followed him past the swaying barges, straining at their moorings. Listening to the slop of the tide against their hulls, I stopped close to the long curving planking of the *Emily*, thrilled my dream of sailing on her might one day come true.

Sam clambered over the gunnel, disappearing down the ladder into the hold. I stood on the quay, looking up at the *Emily* and imagining what life as a waterman would be like. Anxious to find out what was happening, I climbed over the gunnel, down the ladder into the hold, and heard a voice I recognised.

Sam was talking to a man standing in the doorway of the cabin. In the light of a lantern hanging above the door, I saw a dark, hawk like face with a fierce hooked nose. He was wearing fine woollen breeches, a jacket with many buttons, and muddy riding boots.

It was the stranger I'd seen talking to Isaac Whitlock in the yard of *The Tumbling Sailor,* the man even Isaac had seemed afraid of. He was staring in my direction and I backed away in fear.

15

Dangerous Heights

I turned, scrambled up the ladder from the hold, and threw myself over the gunnel. Leaping onto the quay, I ran as fast as I could, the smack of my boots loud on the cobbles.

All the time I expected to hear angry shouts and running footsteps behind me. Daring at last to look behind me, I was startled to see no one was following me. The only sound was my heavy breathing and the loud singing from the taproom of the *Sailor*, the sound blown by the wind down the alleyways onto the deserted quay.

I'd escaped, but I was still scared someone might be after me, creeping behind me in the dark shadows where the moonlight didn't reach. Looking for somewhere to hide, I stopped close to the warehouse wall beside the slipway and peered back along the quay.

I was hoping to see Sam and I waited for him a long time but he didn't come. Deciding I daren't risk staying there much

longer, for I was worrying Isaac might still be searching for me, I grew angry with Sam for deserting me. The damp night air was chilling me to the bone. The longer I stayed there the greater the risk of Isaac catching me. I had to do something. I couldn't wait there until morning.

Thinking I'd be safer in the forest, I made up my mind to take the river path and find somewhere to sleep. I waited a bit longer, hoping to see Sam, but he still didn't come. Feeling miserable and lonely, I began to walk slowly past the warehouse when the side door burst open, sending me sprawling onto the cobbles, and I heard a spiteful voice say, 'Got you!'

Long fingernails dug into the back of my neck. Pulled painfully to my feet, I was face to face with the black bearded Isaac Whitlock. I struggled in terror, but he tightened his grip. I saw Lloyd the banksman standing by the door, holding it open. I fought to break free, but Isaac grabbed me by the shoulder and held me tighter still.

He was dragging me into the warehouse. I managed to cling onto the doorframe, kicking wildly. The banksman was shouting at me, trying to pull my fingers from the wood. Then I heard a shout, footsteps running along the quay, and Sam charged head first into Lloyd, knocking him down. With clenched fists, Sam turned to face Isaac and then froze. Isaac had his arm round my chest. He was holding a knife at my throat.

'Come any nearer and I'll kill him,' Isaac hissed, his voice cold and venomous.

Sam took a step forward, and then he hesitated, looking for some way to free me. Isaac shouted at him to keep back. There was a sharp burning pain as he pressed the knife edge into my neck. I saw the banksman scramble to his feet. He was behind Sam, a large cobblestone in his fist.

'Look out, Sam!' I shouted, but I was too late. Lloyd flung the stone. Sam staggered forward and sank onto his knees. Without a sound, he pitched face down on the quay.

'Don't just stand there looking at him, you useless windbag,' Isaac snarled at the banksman. 'Grab his feet. Hide him before anyone sees him!'

Squealing with fright, the banksman struggled to hold open the door and drag Sam's heavy body into the warehouse. Isaac followed him, still with the knife at my throat. In a pool of moonlight spilling across the brick floor, I saw Sam lying horribly still.

'What are we going to do? Is he dead? Do you think I've

killed him?' the banksman muttered, wringing his pudgy hands together and bending over Sam.

'Shut your whining. Lock the door. Find some rope to tie them up – be quick about it,' Isaac snarled.

Giving a squeal of terror, Lloyd turned the key in the warehouse door. Then he disappeared into the one of the narrow alleyways between heaps of tea chests, huge iron cooking pots, and barrels of wine and cider. After what sounded like much frantic searching, he returned with a length of twine and held it out to Isaac.

'What do you expect me to do with it, you fool? Tie his hands and feet while I hold him,' Isaac snarled. He spun me round, the knife not far from my throat. I felt the banksman's hands tremble as he roughly tied my hands behind my back. Then Isaac pressed hard on my head, forcing me to sit on the floor while Lloyd tied the rope as tight as he could round my ankles.

'What are you going to do with them?' the banksman cried, struggling to tie Sam's wrists and feet together.

Isaac found a piece of filthy rag, tore off a piece, and stuffed it into my mouth so viciously that I thought I would choke. Then wrapping the rest of the rag round my jaw, he tied it behind my head so I couldn't make a sound.

The banksman tried to push some rag into Sam's mouth, but

he couldn't get his jaws open. 'I think – I think he's dead!' he cried fearfully.

'Well, if he isn't, he soon will be,' Isaac said.

The banksman's eyes looked wide and fearful in the moonlight. He nervously prodded Sam with his foot, recoiling in horror when Sam didn't move. 'He seems to have stopped breathing,' he cried.

I felt sick in my stomach to think of what they'd done to Sam. I wanted to yell at them but I couldn't because of the dirty rag.

'If he's dead it'll be easy for you to dump him in the river,' Isaac said. 'Help me, you fool, don't just stand there!'

I watched in silent misery as they dragged Sam down one of the alleyways towards the back of the warehouse, the heels of his boots scraping the brick floor. Then not long after, they came back for me, dragged me between rows of boxes and barrels, and dumped me not far from Sam.

'We'll leave them here till I've finished with that double-crossing Yates. I don't trust him to give us our share, says he didn't get a fair price at Wenlock,' Isaac snorted. 'No one will be here till morning. We'll dump them in the river 'fore first light.'

'But... but won't they float? Won't someone see them?' the banksman said. His voice sounded higher and more nervous than ever.

'We'll weigh them down with something heavy. Go get the cart – you'll need it to carry them down to the river.'

'I can't do it on my own,' the banksman whined.

'Just get the cart,' Isaac snarled. 'I'm going to speak to that thieving Yates.'

He disappeared down one of the alleyways with the banksman trotting after him. I heard the side door of the warehouse opening and closing, and the rattle of the chain. Then the sound of their footsteps on the cobbles grew less and I wriggled frantically until I could sit up with my back against a tea chest.

I kept looking at Sam, but he lay horribly still. Silent tears ran down my face and soaked into the rag tight round my head. It was my fault Sam had died. If I hadn't told him about Isaac, and Sam hadn't been so friendly and kind, he'd still be alive. I just wanted him to be Sam again. Not leave me there on my own, waiting for Isaac to come back and throw me in the river.

16

A Ghost in the Warehouse

I lay on the damp brick floor, looking at poor Sam in the moonlight and worrying what would happen to my mum and sisters if Dad never came back and I was gone. Shivering at the

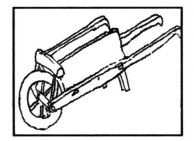

thought of ending my days at the bottom of the Severn, I listened to the slightest sound on the quay. How long would it be before the men came back for me?

Dreading to hear the squeaking wheels of the cart, I struggled with the ropes binding my wrists and ankles. But they were so tight it was useless. Every moment that passed made me more fearful. I thought I heard the cart several times, but no one came.

Then angry with myself for sitting there, just waiting for them to return and drown me, I had an idea. I might be able to hide in a corner somewhere. Then in the morning, when the watermen opened the warehouse, they would find me.

I bent my knees, pressed my feet on the floor, and tried to shuffle along. It was difficult with my hands tied behind me and I didn't get far. Sam was lying across the narrow passageway. Full of despair, I was trying to turn round and find another way out of the alley, when I heard a slight sound and jumped in fright. Afraid Isaac was coming back, I waiting, trembling with fear, but I heard nothing. Thinking I'd been mistaken, I heard the noise again. A sort of soft scuffling. This time it was a little louder.

I looked fearfully about, trying to see where it was coming from. I could see nothing moving in the shadows. Then I heard it again. My skin crawled with fright. I thought it might be a rat. I'd be helpless to defend myself with my hands and feet tied together. The thought of a rat jumping on my chest and biting my face made me sick with terror.

I began to imagine there was a rat crouched behind one of the boxes, waiting for the moment to scuttle across the floor and spring at me. Then the scuffling noise came again. This time it was louder. It seemed to be coming closer. I cried out, but with the foul rag stuffed in my mouth, all I could do was make a gurgling sound.

There was the terrible scuffling noise again. I was panicking

155

so much it took me some time before I realised the sound was coming from Sam's direction. His foot was moving. I stared in horror, thinking his ghost was rising up to haunt me. In the shafts of moonlight, I saw the body lift its head. It turned to look at me with unseeing eyes. I was so scared I could hardly breathe. I was shrinking away from it, when the apparition burst out laughing.

'You should have seen your face,' Sam cried, 'ouch - it hurts to laugh. It was a mighty hard whack the banksman gave me. Did you think me dead? Nah, I'm tougher than that,' he chortled.

I tried to shout at him, tell him it wasn't funny. That I'd nearly died of fright. All I could do was grunt furiously. This made him laugh more. He grinned at me, rolled onto his side, and curled up into a very tight ball with his knees under his chin.

'Watch,' he said. He brought his tightly bound hands from under his body, slipped them over his feet, and uncurled. I stared in amazement, for his hands now rested across his belly. Then sitting up, he shuffled towards me. With his wrists still tied together, he used his fingers, tugged the filthy cloth from round my head, and pulled the disgusting rag out of my mouth.

'I thought you were a ghost,' I croaked, my mouth dry and my throat stinging. 'The banksman said you were dead!'

Sam laughed a long warm chuckling sound. 'Thought so, the way you were looking at me, your eyes got bigger and bigger.

Turn round. Let's see if I can rid you of these ropes.'

I felt him tugging at my wrists. Then he said, 'Can't do it,' and I heard him cursing.

He was silent for what seemed a long while. Desperately wondering what he was up to, I felt something sharp dig into my wrist. 'That hurt! What are you doing?' I shouted.

'Keep still or I'll really hurt you,' he said. 'I knew it would come in handy. I saved the bit of broken blade I found in the coal shed. It's hard holding it – keep still or I'll cut you.'

'That's no good,' I cried. 'It's blunt, you'll never saw through the ropes with–'

'It's better than nothing,' he muttered, 'just keep still.'

I waited nervously, feeling the blade rubbing against the rope around my wrists. I could hear Sam muttering to himself. From time to time, the point of the blade dug into me and I cried out. Sam took no notice and kept on sawing.

'Why did you run off?' he said. I was too afraid the blade would cut me to reply. The longer he took the more scared I was, thinking the men would soon return. I shouted angrily, telling him to hurry up, when I felt the rope drop away from my wrists. Tugging frantically at the knotted rope round my ankles, I managed to free one foot, then the other, and struggled to stand.

The pain was awful, but I stamped my feet. Violently rubbing my arms until I could feel them again, I tugged at Sam's tied wrists.

'I ran because the master's one of the men I saw in the yard at *The Tumbling Sailor* – he was the man who gave Isaac the warehouse key,' I said.

'I always thought Yates was up to no good – hurry up before they come back. Get the rope off me.'

Once Sam's hands were free, it didn't take him long to pull the rope from his ankles. Then hobbling across the floor as the blood came back into his feet, he said, 'Let's get out of here.' He led the way to the side door, but we couldn't get it open. The huge doors onto the slipway were locked, too.

'We could climb through one of those windows,' I said. I pointed to where moonlight was streaming through a row of small iron-framed windows, high up in the brickwork in the back wall of the warehouse. 'The sills look deep enough to climb onto.'

'Dunna be daft. How are we going to get up there?'

'There're enough boxes, we could pile them against a wall.'

Sam shook his head. I took no notice of him and started to drag a tea chest across the floor. When he saw what I was up to, he began to help me. We worked furiously, lifting three wooden chests on top of each other, but they were heavy. It was impossible to lift another on top of those already stacked against the wall, even for Sam. We had to use smaller bundles, bales of different sizes, and soon we had a wobbling tower.

'What happens if the men come back before we've finished?' Sam asked. Gasping for breath, he climbed the tottering heap, struggling to place another odd-looking bundle on top of it.

'Be careful, the lot's going to fall,' I cried. I held my breath as he climbed down again.

'I think you can reach the window sill now – you try,' he said.

I'm afraid of heights, but I was lighter than Sam was and not so clumsy. I climbed slowly, trying not to look down, and found my head level with the windowsill. 'The sill *is* fairly deep,' I called down to him, 'I think I can climb onto it.'

With trembling hands, I snatched at the iron bar in the middle of a window frame. Pulling myself up, I knelt on the brickwork. I was scared the bar would snap and I'd go hurtling to the floor below. But the row of small windows stretching along the back wall had a long sill beneath them. It was easy for me to crawl along it.

I tried lifting a window latch, but it wouldn't move. 'The windows won't open,' I cried in alarm, 'the window latches are rusted.'

'Won't be long,' Sam muttered.

Crouched on the sill, terrified of falling, it seemed a long time before I saw Sam's freckled face grinning up at me. He held an iron bolt in his hand and said, 'Will this do?'

I leaned down as far as I dared. Taking it from him, I hammered at a window latch until it broke, scared Isaac would hear the noise I was making. Then thrusting the window open, I clung with both hands to the frame, looked down, and quickly

drew my head in again. 'It's a long drop down the side of the building and there's only a narrow path along the edge of the river. The path goes to the slipway – but we'd need a rope to get down to it.'

'I'm sure I've seen rope somewhere,' Sam said.

'Be quick,' I cried.

'Won't be long,' he said cheerfully. He kept his word. He was soon back again. Climbing up the dangerously wobbling heap, he dragged a length of hawser behind him.

I held my breath as he lifted one end of it up towards me. 'It's coming untwisted in places,' he said.

'Never mind that. Quick, give it to me before Isaac comes back!'

Using all his strength, he heaved on the hawser, straining to take the weight of it as he passed the end up to me. Balancing on the ledge, I struggled to tie the hawser to the middle bar of the window, all the time petrified I'd fall. Sam lifted the rope bit by bit. I pushed it through the window and it dropped through the opening to the river below.

'It doesn't reach the path,' I said, 'at least I don't think so.' I hated looking down. It seemed worse than going down the pit. At least in the wagon I'd had someone with me, even if the last time it had been only poor Billy.

'There's nothing to worry about,' Sam said. 'I've been higher than this on the *Emily*. You'll be all right, Josh, just dunna look down.'

Pushing open the small window as far as it would go, I shuffled along the sill, making room for Sam to climb up beside me. Pulling on the rope to see if it would hold him, Sam lowered himself through the window, hooked his feet round the rope, and then he was gone.

Moments later, I heard him say in a very loud whisper, 'Come on, there's only a bit of a drop to the path. You'll be all right.'

Trying to pluck up enough courage to follow him, I heard a sound behind me that echoed hollowly through the building. Someone was opening the side door of the warehouse. There were footsteps coming along an alleyway. I leaned desperately

161

out of the window, looking down to the dark river below.

The boxes under me were wobbling. Isaac was climbing towards me. Bellowing to the banksman to run to the slipway and stop me escaping, he reached up to grab my foot. Frozen with fear, I looked down to the river.

Sam yelled, 'Come on, Josh!'

Isaac's hand touched my boot. With a shriek, I seized hold of the rope, squeezed through the window, and slid. The path was coming closer, I felt the hawser jerk violently, and looking up I saw Isaac sliding rapidly down the rope towards me.

17

A Promise Made

Isaac's boots were close to my head. He was kicking, trying to knock me off the rope. In a desperate effort to keep away from his feet I lurched sideways, making the rope swing wildly. He tried to stamp on my head and I ducked to avoid him. The rope twisted violently, swinging so wildly about I feared I'd be smashed against the warehouse wall.

Isaac clamped his legs tight round the rope, holding on with one hand, and reached down to grab my hair. I pulled away from him, leaving lumps of hair in his clawing fingers, my scalp burning. Again he kicked out savagely, trying to knock me into the river. I swung away from him and this time felt the rope unravelling. Looking up in terror, I saw the hawser slip from the middle bar of the window and I fell with the rope still clutched in my hands.

I hit the path. Isaac landed with a terrible whack beside me.

Bruised and shocked, I scrambled to my feet. Freeing myself from the coils of heavy rope, I fled along the path. Sam was standing on the slipway, yelling something. I glanced over my shoulder and saw Isaac close behind me, a knife clasped in his hand.

Reaching the end of the path, I leapt onto the slipway. Sam shoved me out of his way and ran at Isaac. The knife sliced into Sam's arm. He cried out, I saw a dark stain spreading on his sleeve. Backing away from Isaac, Sam ripped off his jacket, wrapping it round his arm and hand for protection.

Isaac was like a maddened dog, trying to strike again. Sam dodged about, keeping just out of reach. I looked desperately for anything to use as a weapon. Seeing a piece of wood on the cobbles, I snatched it up. Sam grasped Isaac's wrist, trying to shake the knife from his hand. Sam was strong, but Isaac was heavier and stronger. The knife was close to Sam's neck.

With a cry of rage, I ran at Isaac, striking him on the back of the head with the lump of wood. He staggered. The knife flew out of his hand, clattering on the cobbles. Sam dived towards it, but Isaac was quicker. Snatching it up, he lunged at Sam. I ran at Isaac, but before I could strike again, a wild shout rang out. Farm workers armed with billhooks, scythes, and pitchforks, were running along the quay towards me.

Isaac saw them too. He hesitated, then turned and ran. The men sprinted after him. One man, faster then the others, brought him down. Isaac fought like a wild animal. It took three men to wrestle the knife from him. I was watching them drag him away, when Sam swayed and looked about to fall.

He'd dropped his jacket on the cobbles and blood dripped from his arm. He looked so pale in the moonlight his freckles were like some strange disease. Remembering Mum's cloth in my pocket, I pulled it out. Tying it as tight as I could round his wound, I shouted for help. Two farm workers came over and led Sam along the quay towards *The Tumbling Sailor*.

I saw white hair, silvered in the moonlight. Sir Edmund Atterley, the owner of the magnificent stallion, was standing by the doorway of the inn. Ordering the men to take Sam into the inn, he strode off down the quay. I followed Sam as the farm workers helped him down a stone passageway into the parlour.

I waited in the doorway, looking at the beautiful furniture, soft rugs, and the lamp light glowing on the polished surface of the table by the window. I felt too dirty to enter the room. Waiting till the men had lowered Sam into a comfortable armchair close to fire and had left us alone, I walked over to him but he'd closed his eyes.

He was still a horrible colour under the dust and dirt clinging to him. He was clutching him arm, his face full of pain. Alarmed at the sight of him, I was going to find help when the parlour door opened. A man came into the room and I gave a sigh of relief. I recognised the chimney pot hat of the Coalport doctor.

'Can you help my friend Sam? He's wounded bad,' I cried. Then remembering the last time I'd seen the chimney pot hat was at the pithead, I gasped with sudden fear. 'Are the men in the mine safe?' I said.

The doctor took no notice of me. Bending over, he roughly removed Mum's cloth that I'd wrapped round Sam's arm. Then he called for water, and it wasn't long before a girl hurried into the parlour carrying a basin of water and clean cloths. Then kneeling beside Sam the doctor ripped away his sleeve and washed the wound, removed a nasty looking needle from his bag, and while he stitched, I quickly looked away.

'The cut isn't too deep,' he said, finishing his stitching and wrapping Sam's arm in a clean cloth. Then looking sternly at Sam's dirty face and clothes, he shook his head, telling him that the wound would heal if he kept it clean.

When the doctor left the parlour, I hurried after him, carrying the basin to the kitchen. I was desperate to catch up with him and ask him about Dad before he left the inn, but I was too late. Bitterly disappointed, I was on my way back along the narrow passageway when I saw the door to the taproom open and looked inside.

Men seated on benches were supping ale, and I hurried up to a man on a settle, close by the door, and asked if he knew what had happened to the men trapped in the mine. He shook his head at me and returned to his drinking. I tried to ask someone else, but I was shouted at and told to be gone. Returning miserably to the parlour, I found Sir Edmund seated beside the hearth talking to Sam. To my surprise, Sam looked better and he was laughing.

'Sam tells me you are thinking about being a waterman,' Sir Edmund said, turning in his high-backed chair to look at me. His thin lined face creased in a smile as he invited me to sit on a stool beside the fire.

'That – that was before,' I stammered. I settled cautiously on the edge of the stool, worried in case my dirty clothing left a stain. 'Before Isaac was caught, Sir. Now I shall take up the pick and earn a man's wage. I need to pay rent for our cottage, so Mum and my sisters won't be turned onto the street and be sent to the workhouse.'

'Do you want to take up the pick?' he asked with a frown.

'I have no choice.' I said, though my heart was already sinking at the thought of it.

'What if I told you that there is no need for you to do that?' he

167

said.

Puzzled by his words, I saw Sam grinning at me and looking very smug. Wondering what the man had said to him, I was jealous of Sam's secret and that he knew more than I did.

'I don't understand, Sir,' I said.

'I offered a reward for the capture of the thieves, for they were stealing *my* possessions. You and Sam led me to the villains. The reward is yours to share, for you've earned it. The money should keep your family in rent for a long time to come.' He smiled and looked at Sam. 'It was my wife's dress material you used to bandage your hand. First your hand, now your arm. Don't make a habit of it, I have need of you.'

Sam grinned, despite his wound, and muttered his thanks. I was more puzzled than ever. I wondered what this man might need from Sam and longed to hear.

'I'd never have caught the thieves if you hadn't told me about Isaac, and my woodsman,' he said, turning to me. 'We thought it was the work of the bow haulers, but this stealing was on a bigger scale. Too well organised. The reward money will keep you from work in the pit, if that's what you want, but I've other ideas. I'm in need of a groom for my new hunter, someone who can control Thunder. He's a handful, I'm sure you would agree, but you have a way with the horse. I think you could handle him.

168

What do you say? Will you do it?'

For a moment, I couldn't believe my good fortune. It would be a wonderful life, groom to that beautiful stallion. Then I remembered, and sadly shook my head. 'I would like to do it more than anything, Sir, but I can't. Dad is trapped in the mine. I must look after my mum and sisters.'

'Is your father one of the miners at Blists Hill? I've heard they've broken through the tunnel and brought out some of the men alive.'

'Was my dad one of those saved?' I cried. 'Is he amongst the injured?'

'I'm afraid I don't know.'

'His name's Hale, George Hale, Sir.'

'Hale... I think I know that name.'

I waited, longing for him to say more. I wanted to cry out with disappointment when at last he said, 'Hmmm... I can't be sure. I think my wife had a maid – a good, hard working girl. My wife was fond of her. She married someone called Hale. What was your mother's name before she married?'

I could hardly bring myself to answer him, I was desperate to hear news of my dad, but trying to hide my misery I said, 'Carter – her name was Carter, Sir.'

'Yes, that's the very one. We had a maid called Carter. My

wife will be pleased to hear of her. You have sisters? Perhaps that shall not be a problem. You and your family could move into the old shepherd's cottage. The one you seemed to be living in when you were devouring my carrots.'

He laughed quietly at his own joke. Then he said, as if talking to himself alone, 'I'll have the roof repaired. The door and windows mended.' Then he turned to me. 'There'll be enough money from the reward to buy anything else you need. Your sisters can work in the dairy. I'm sure my wife will be eager to have your mother in her employ again.'

'But my dad–'

'Your father... well, if he's injured he can move into the cottage with you,' he said. 'If he's not, I'm sure we can find work for him on the home farm. What do you say to that? Or is your heart really set on taking up the pick?'

'I thank you, Sir,' I said, trying to sound grateful. It was hard to hide my disappointment there was no news of Dad. 'I thank you for Mum and my sisters too. Maria hates sieving the coal on the pit bank. She would love to work in a dairy. But – but what will happen to Isaac?'

'He and his friends will be shipped to the Colonies. The master of the *Emily* planned the robberies, gave Isaac the key to the warehouse. Then he rode to Wenlock to arrange the sale of

170

my goods. When my men catch him, he and his friends will disappear forever. You'll not be bothered with them again!'

Suddenly realising that I had been so busy thinking about my own worries I had forgotten Sam, I said, 'Please, what is going to happen to Sam? Now he is wounded and the *Emily* has no master?'

'I'm thinking of giving the job of master to Griffiths, when he returns from Jackfield. That's why Yates let him spend time with his family. Didn't want him to know about the thieving, but I shall need to find a new second mate to serve on her.'

'But Sam is second mate, Sir,' I cried in alarm. 'The doctor said his arm would heal and–'

'You've no need to worry,' Sir Edmund said. He smiled at Sam who grinned back. 'He'll sail with the *Emily* when she leaves for Worcester – but as first mate. I need people on the *Emily* I can trust. Griffiths will find someone to work alongside him. I'm thinking of taking on a new boy. I was given the idea that you might want to be a waterman, but I think you'll be happier as groom, for Thunder seems to like you.'

I could hardly believe our good luck. I was busy wondering if there would be enough money to buy Drummer, and have the grumpy old pony with me again, when the door of the parlour opened and a serving girl entered. She place a large platter on the table by the window and I saw a roast leg of mutton, all sizzling hot with the juices from the pan. I looked eagerly as another girl brought in a huge pie decorated with pastry leaves, and a dish piled high with roast potatoes. It all smelled so good. There was a dish of carrots. Sam and me looked quickly at each other and tried not to laugh.

Then the girls returned with a slab of cheese, a bowl of cream, a dish of cooked apples, and a jug of ale. I think Sam was like me, hoping for some of the leavings. To our astonishment, the owner of the *Emily* waved his hand towards the wonderful food on the table and walked towards the door.

'Help yourselves, you've earned it,' he said. 'I must thank my men from the home farm and see they are provided for – they did a good night's work, apprehending Isaac Whitlock, and the innkeeper. I'm sure they'll find Yates and Lloyd before long, so you'll have no need to worry.' Then nodding to Sam, and then at me, he left the parlour while we stammered our awkward thanks.

I led the way to the table. Cutting thick slices of mutton for each of us, and some of the meat pie, I put the food on our plates. Then I piled up the buttered potatoes on Sam's plate, though neither of us wanted carrots. I gave him more food than me because he'd earned it. I thought he needed lots because of his wound, but there was more than enough for us both.

We ate and ate. I'd never tasted anything so good in my life. There was so much food we couldn't eat it all. Then after we'd started on the dish of apples, gobbled down most of it, and shared the jug of cream, we supped our mugs of ale. I was so full and comfortable I forgot my dirty clothes, and we settled in the armchairs close to the fire.

There was a long silence, both of us feeling warm and sleepy. Then I looked across at Sam, at his poor bandaged arm, and said, 'You saved my life again.'

'Well, I wunna make a habit of it, if you promise not to get into more trouble, that is.'

'Thanks anyway... I'm sorry you are hurt, Sam.'

'Dunna fret,' Sam said. 'You'll come an' see me again? That's if you're not too high and mighty. Now you'll be riding that black stallion, an' you'll be a landowner with a cottage an'

all.'

'High and mighty yourself. You're to be first mate on the *Emily* and master one day, I don't doubt.'

'We'll sail down to Bristol together before long, won't we?' Sam said. 'You promise now.'

I looked through the window of the inn. In the light from the oil lamps along the quay, I saw the *Emily Grey* rising gently at her moorings and thought of Dad. He'd longed to be a waterman again, I'd had a grand idea of one day being the master of the *Emily*, but now all I wanted was to find Dad safe.

Then remembering Sam was waiting for an answer, I looked at his kindly freckled face, then at the *Emily* and said, 'Yes, Sam, I don't know when, but that's a promise. One day I'll sail with you to Bristol.'

Bibliography

B. S. Trinder, *'The Industrial Revolution in Shropshire'*, (1973).

Arthur Raistrick, *'Dynasty of Iron Founders'*, (1989 © Ironbridge Gorge Museum Trust).

B. Bracegirdle & P. H. Miles, '*The Darbys and the Ironbridge Gorge'*, (1974).

Alan Gallop, '*Children of the Dark'*, (life and death underground in Victoria's England), (2003)

C. S. Johnson, '*The Rebuilding of the Severn Trow Spry'*, (1978)

Royal Commission on Children's Employment (Mines), (1842)

(1850) *Articles written by reporter Charles Dickens for 'Household Worlds - interviews with miners regarding accidents in coal mines'.*

From the Shropshire Books Series, Editor Adrian Pearce, *'Mining in Shropshire'*, (1995)

Rachel Labouchere, '*Abiah Darby'*, (1988)

About the Author

Carole Anne Carr has had a varied life, working as a teenager in a bank in Zimbabwe, then returning to England to become deputy head of a primary school. After early retirement, there were many careers. After working as an actress, she then set up her own art and craft business, trained for three years to hold the Office of Reader in the Church of England, and then became a full time writer of children's fiction. Living in Shropshire, she writes historical fiction for older children, and writes and illustrates books for younger readers.

She will shortly be completing a second book in the Ironbridge Gorge Series, *River Dark* and hopes to begin *Kendra*, the second of the *Wolf Series*. Then she will continue to write her way around her much-loved historical sites in Shropshire - places she visited when taking children on environmental study trips for many, many years.

Books by Carole Anne Carr

First Wolf
Book One - Wolf Series

Little Boy Good-for-Nothing and the Shongololo

Thin Time
Book One - Task Bearer Series

Available Soon

River Dark
Book Two - Ironbridge Gorge Series

Kendra
Book Two - Wolf Series